Atonement Trail

LAUREL VALLEY

LILIANA HART

Also by Liliana Hart

JJ Graves Mystery Series

Dirty Little Secrets

A Dirty Shame

Dirty Rotten Scoundrel

Down and Dirty

Dirty Deeds

Dirty Laundry

Dirty Money

A Dirty Job

Dirty Devil

Playing Dirty

Dirty Martini

Dirty Dozen

Dirty Minds

Dirty Weekend

Dirty Looks

Dirty Liars

Dirty Valentine

Addison Holmes Mystery Series

Whiskey Rebellion

Whiskey Sour

Whiskey For Breakfast

Whiskey, You're The Devil

Whiskey on the Rocks

Whiskey Tango Foxtrot

Whiskey and Gunpowder

Whiskey Lullaby

The Scarlet Chronicles

Bouncing Betty

Hand Grenade Helen

Front Line Francis

The Harley and Davidson Mystery Series

The Farmer's Slaughter

A Tisket a Casket

I Saw Mommy Killing Santa Claus

Get Your Murder Running

Deceased and Desist

Malice in Wonderland

Tequila Mockingbird

Gone With the Sin

Grime and Punishment

Blazing Rattles

A Salt and Battery

Curl Up and Dye

First Comes Death Then Comes Marriage

Box Set 1

Box Set 2

Box Set 3

The Gravediggers

The Darkest Corner

Gone to Dust

Say No More

Laurel Valley

Tribulation Pass

Redemption Road

Midnight Clear

Forgiveness River

Atonement Trail

Chapter One

OCTOBER MORNINGS IN LAUREL VALLEY ARRIVED
like old friends—familiar, comforting, and
carrying stories in every shadow. Dylan Flanagan
left her apartment above Millicent's Antiques at
five thirty, when the town belonged to ghosts and
memories and people like her who preferred their
solitude served with sunrise.

The cobblestone streets gleamed with dew,
treacherous under her worn boots but beautiful in
the way that dangerous things often were. The
Bavarian-style buildings stood like something from
a children's book—peaked roofs and painted shutters, window boxes that would soon transition
from autumn mums to winter greens, every detail
carefully maintained to sell the illusion that this
had always been an Alpine village rather than a

mining town that had learned to survive by becoming something else entirely.

Dylan pulled her jacket tighter against the mountain air that carried hints of woodsmoke and the coming winter. Five years of these morning walks, and she still wasn't sure if she was walking toward something or away from it. Maybe both. Maybe neither. Maybe just walking because movement felt like progress even when you were traveling in circles.

Heavenly Delights Bakery sat on the corner like a promise of warmth, its curved glass windows dark but welcoming. Rose always left a thermos outside for the early shift workers—the ones who kept Laurel Valley running while the tourists slept. Black coffee, strong enough to wake the dead, with a trust box for payment that had never once come up short in the thirty years Rose had been doing this.

Dylan poured her coffee into her travel mug, left her three dollars in the box, and continued down Main Street. The Reading Nook's restored stained-glass window caught the first hint of dawn, throwing prisms across the sidewalk like scattered hopes. Sophie O'Hara had rebuilt after the fire two years ago, and the bookstore was now the crown jewel of downtown, proof that broken things could be made beautiful again. Sometimes.

Past Raven's boutique with its mannequins dressed for lives Dylan would never lead—cashmere and confidence, designer bags that cost more than her monthly rent. Past The Lampstand, where Simone O'Hara would already be in the kitchen, starting the pot roast that would simmer all day, filling downtown with the scent of home cooking that made tourists believe they'd found authentic mountain life.

The town square stood empty, the gazebo that hosted summer concerts now decorated with pumpkins and corn stalks for the Harvest Festival next week. The old skating rink had been drained for the season, leaves gathering in its basin like collected memories. Come December, it would be filled again, and the massive Christmas tree would go up, and Laurel Valley would transform into the kind of place that existed in snow globes and holiday movies.

Five years she'd been walking these streets. Five years of watching the town change with the seasons while she remained exactly the same— suspended in amber, preserved like one of the antiques in Millicent's shop window.

The envelope in her jacket pocket pressed against her ribs with each step. Pacific Custom Restoration's latest offer, delivered yesterday with a deadline that felt more like a countdown. Marcus Rowan had even included photos of the shop—pristine bays, state-of-the-art equipment, a paint booth that made her current setup look like a child's crayon box.

Her phone buzzed—speak of the devil. She let it go to voicemail. Marcus would call again. And again. Men like him always did, unable to understand that not everyone was motivated by the same things that drove them.

By the time she reached The Pinnacle Garage, the sky had shifted from black to deep purple, the mountains emerging from darkness like slowly developing photographs. The garage occupied a converted warehouse on the edge of downtown's deliberately maintained charm, its modern lines a stark contrast to the Bavarian fantasy behind her.

She unlocked the side door with her key, breathing in the familiar scent of motor oil and metal, possibility and purpose. The lights flickered on, revealing her kingdom—six bays, each one currently occupied, tools arranged with military precision, the concrete floor so clean you could perform surgery on it.

Her corner called to her—the 1970 Plymouth Barracuda she'd been resurrecting for three months sat there like a purple jewel, waiting for the final touches that would bring it back to life. She'd always been able to see what it could be beneath the rust and neglect.

She ran her hand along the hood, checking the paint she'd applied yesterday. Perfect. Plum Crazy purple, exactly as Chrysler had made it in 1970, with a white racing stripe that ran down the center like lightning frozen in time. Mrs. Morrison would cry when she saw it—they always did when they saw their past restored, made better than memory.

The irony wasn't lost on her. She could resurrect dead cars but couldn't seem to fix her own life. Couldn't stop herself from checking the time, knowing that in exactly one hour and forty-five minutes, Aidan O'Hara would walk through that door, and her carefully controlled world would tilt on its axis the way it did every morning at seven fifteen.

Dylan grabbed her creeper and slid under the Barracuda, checking the fuel line one more time. The undercarriage told its own story—decades of Montana winters, salt scarred and weather beaten, now restored to better than new. She'd sweet-talked old-timers from here to New Mexico for original parts, haunted junkyards like a grieving relative, learned the exact pressure required to wet sand paint until it became liquid color.

Her phone rang again. This time she pulled herself out from under the car and answered, if only to stop the insistent buzzing.

"It's not even seven, Marcus."

"Dylan, finally." His voice carried that particular Seattle intensity—urgent, caffeinated, important. "I've been trying to reach you for days."

"I've been working." She wiped her hands on a shop rag, already knowing where this conversation was heading. "The answer's still the same."

"You haven't heard the new offer."

"I don't need to—"

"Ten thousand signing bonus." He paused, letting the number settle between them like a challenge. "Plus full relocation, your own restoration bay, and first pick of projects. You'd be lead specialist, Dylan. The work you'd be doing— museum-quality restorations, cars that belong in collections. Not just keeping tourists' rentals running."

Dylan closed her eyes. Ten thousand dollars. That was a lot of money. She could stop checking her bank balance before buying groceries. Could maybe even think about a future that consisted of more than just getting through each month.

"I'm driving down today," Marcus continued. "I'll be there by noon. Just give me an hour to show you what we're offering. You're too talented to be hidden away in a tourist town."

"Marcus—"

"I'm already in Spokane. Noon, Dylan. The Lampstand. Just lunch and conversation."

He hung up before she could protest, leaving her standing alone in the garage that suddenly felt smaller than it had five minutes ago.

Through the open bay door, she could see Laurel Valley waking up. The sun had crested the mountains now, turning the town into something from a postcard—perfect, contained, impossibly beautiful. Soon the streets would fill with tourists clutching cameras and lattes, searching for the authentic mountain experience that Laurel Valley had perfected selling them.

She returned to the Barracuda, focusing on the engine that gleamed like jewelry under the hood. This was what she was good at—taking something broken and making it whole, bringing the dead back to life, creating beauty from rust and neglect.

The rumble of a truck in the parking lot made her look up. Seven o'clock—Ralph arriving for his shift, right on time. Soon the garage would fill with noise and work and the comfortable chaos of a business day.

Dylan tucked the envelope back in her pocket as Ralph burst through the door, his energy preceding him like a wave.

"Morning, sunshine!" he called out, his voice echoing in the empty space. His walrus mustache twitched with amusement. "Beat me here again. You trying to make the rest of us look bad?"

"Sleep is overrated," Dylan said, falling into their familiar banter.

Ralph was somewhere north of fifty, had been turning wrenches for thirty years, and treated everyone in the garage like they were part of his extended family. His salt-and-pepper hair was already escaping from under his cap.

"You finish the Morrison car?" He came over to admire the Barracuda, letting out a low whistle. "Man, that paint job is perfect. She's going to flip."

"That's the idea."

"You ever think about opening your own restoration shop?" Ralph asked, running his hand along the car's lines. "You're too good to be working for someone else."

The envelope seemed to burn in her pocket. "Maybe someday."

"You've been saying that for two years." He grabbed his coveralls from his locker. "Danny and I have a bet going. He thinks you'll be here forever. I think you've got bigger plans."

If only he knew she'd been saying maybe someday in every shop she'd ever worked in. It was easier than saying the truth—that she didn't know how to stop moving long enough to build something permanent.

"Speaking of Danny, where is he?" she asked, deflecting.

"Running late. His baby kept him up all night. Teething or something." Ralph stroked his mustache sympathetically. "Thank God my kids are grown. I'd forgotten what those sleepless nights were like until he started coming in looking like the walking dead."

Dylan smiled despite herself. Ralph had three grown kids and five grandkids, and his toolbox was plastered with their pictures. Roots. Family. The kind of permanence that both terrified and fascinated her.

The bell on the wall phone rang, shrill in the morning quiet. Dylan answered it, half listening to Mrs. Morrison confirming the four o'clock pickup time for the Barracuda. Her voice was so excited, so full of anticipation for the surprise she was giving her husband.

"He's going to cry," Mrs. Morrison confided. "He sold that car to pay for our daughter's college. Broke his heart, but he never complained. He deserves to have it back."

After Dylan hung up, she stood looking at the Barracuda. A car that had been sold for love, restored for love, given back in love. The kind of story that made her chest ache with want for something she'd never had. Something she'd stopped believing she could have.

At exactly seven fifteen, Aidan O'Hara's truck pulled into the parking lot.

Dylan didn't need to look up to know it was him. She knew the sound of that engine like she knew her own heartbeat—a 1967 F-100 he'd restored himself, painted deep blue like the lake in summer. She knew he'd park in the same spot he always did, three spaces from the door. Knew he'd check his phone before getting out, probably deleting messages from women he'd disappointed by not calling back.

Five years of this routine. Five years of pretending she didn't time her coffee breaks to coincide with his. Five years of casually asking Ralph about Aidan's weekend plans, then making sure she had somewhere else to be when he mentioned dinner reservations at Lakeside Lodge or drinks at the new wine bar that catered to the resort crowd. Aidan never lacked for company. He was a social creature by nature, the complete opposite of her. Which is why her attraction to him would only ever be a fantasy.

The door opened, and October air swept in, carrying the scent of cedar and mountain air. Aidan moved through the world like he owned it, and maybe he did. The O'Haras were Laurel Valley, their name on half the businesses downtown. They belonged here in a way Dylan never would, their roots so deep they'd become part of the mountain itself.

"Morning, Dylan," he called out, and she had to look up, had to meet those green eyes that made her forget every perfectly logical reason she should take the Seattle job.

"Morning." She kept her voice neutral, professional, safe.

He started toward her bay, that easy stride that ate up ground without seeming to hurry. Five years, and her pulse still did that stupid skip when he smiled at her like they shared a secret. Five years of being quietly, hopelessly in love with a man who went through women like restoration projects—he gave them intense focus until they were fixed, then it was on to the next challenge.

"The Barracuda looks incredible," he said, stopping at a safe distance but still close enough that she could smell his soap—something piney and clean that made her think of mountain mornings. "Morrison's going to lose it."

"That's the idea." Dylan forced herself to focus on the engine, adjusting something that didn't need adjusting.

"Hey, did you get my text about the book club Thursday?" He leaned against the workbench in that way that made his shoulders look broader. "Sophie keeps asking if you're coming. She said you promised and it's time you do something besides spend all your time at the shop."

She had promised, three weeks ago in a moment of weakness when Sophie had been particularly persistent and Dylan had been partic-ularly tired of saying no to everything that might make her feel like she belonged here.

"Yeah, I'll be there," she said.

"Good." His voice carried something different this morning, something that made her look up despite herself. "Sophie's right. Whether you're ready or not, you're part of this community."

Before she could parse what that meant—if it meant anything at all—Danny rushed through the door, baby spit-up on his shoulder and exhaustion written in every line of his face.

"Sorry I'm late," he called out. "The baby was up all night, and then she decided to redecorate my shirt right as I was leaving."

"The joys of parenthood," Ralph said, already launching into a story about his youngest grandkid's soccer game.

Aidan lingered for a moment longer, and Dylan felt the weight of his attention like sunshine —warm, dangerous, impossible to ignore.

"Great job on the Barracuda," he said.

She watched him go, watched him stop to joke with Ralph, to admire Danny's latest baby pictures, to check the schedule in his office. He moved through the garage like he moved through life—confident, comfortable, completely unaware that he was slowly breaking her heart just by existing in the same space.

The envelope in her pocket felt heavier than a transmission.

Less than five hours until lunch, until Marcus would sit across from her at The Lampstand and offer her everything she'd thought she wanted—escape, financial security, a fresh start where nobody knew she was the mechanic who'd been stupid enough to fall for her boss.

Five hours to decide if she was brave enough to stay in a place where she'd always be watching from the sidelines, or smart enough to leave before October became November became another year of loving someone who would never love her back.

Dylan picked up her tools and got back to work, because that's what she did. She fixed things. She made them beautiful. She brought them back to life.

Everything except herself.

Chapter Two

SUNDAY DINNER AT THE O'HARA FARMHOUSE unfolded like a weekly sacrament, complete with its own liturgy of laughter, the passing of dishes like offerings, and Anne O'Hara's pot roast serving as communion—tender enough to convert even the most devoted vegetarian. The farmhouse itself seemed to breathe with contentment, its bones settling into familiar rhythms as five brothers, their wives, and various offspring created the kind of chaos that sounded like home.

Aidan pushed his mashed potatoes around his plate, building and destroying mountain ranges with the distraction of a man whose mind was elsewhere entirely. Two days. Two days since he'd watched Dylan leave for lunch on Friday with that overdressed stranger from Seattle. Two days of the town gossips working overtime, speculation running wild about Dylan Flanagan's mysterious lunch companion.

"You planning to eat those potatoes or just torture them?" Duncan asked from across the table, his artist's eye noting every tell in his brother's posture.

"Leave him alone," Sophie said, though her eyes sparkled with mischief. "He's been in a mood since Friday. Ever since Dylan had lunch with that well-dressed man from Seattle."

The table went quiet for a heartbeat—the kind of quiet that happened when someone had inadvertently struck gold in the conversational mine.

"Well-dressed?" Aidan's voice came out more growl than question.

"Very," Raven confirmed with the satisfaction of someone who'd been waiting for this opening. "Expensive suit, Tesla in the parking lot, looked like he stepped out of a magazine. Rose said they were discussing business, but Dylan was leaning in, really engaged. You know how she usually is with strangers—all walls and distance. But she actually seemed interested in what he had to say."

"Rose says a lot of things," Aidan muttered, stabbing a piece of pot roast with unnecessary force.

"Shannon saw them too," Sophie added, clearly enjoying herself. "Said he was very persistent. Kept pulling out documents, showing her things on his phone. Like he was trying to sell her something. Or recruit her."

Aidan had spent Friday afternoon waiting for Dylan to return from lunch, but when she came back, she'd gone straight to work preparing the Barracuda for delivery. He'd been stuck on a conference call with a parts supplier, and by the time he'd gotten free, Ralph mentioned that Dylan had borrowed his truck to deliver the car to the Morrisons—something about Mrs. Morrison wanting it in their driveway when her husband got home from his golf game. By the time she'd returned and tossed Ralph his keys, Aidan had been pulled into another crisis with the father of a frat boy who didn't know how to drive his new Porsche without grinding the gears, and Dylan had already walked home.

"Maybe it's good for her," Colt said reasonably, his doctor's instincts reading the tension in Aidan's shoulders. "She's been here five years and never really connects with anyone. A woman like that shouldn't be so isolated."

"She's not isolated," Aidan said before he could stop himself. "She has the garage. The town. She has—" *Me*, he almost said, but caught himself.

"A job and an apartment above an antique shop?" Wyatt finished. "That's not a life, that's just existing."

Anne O'Hara watched her middle son with the attention of a mother who recognized a crisis when she saw one. She rose from her chair with the grace of someone who'd been managing male emotions for forty years and disappeared into the butler's pantry.

When she returned, she carried something that made every O'Hara at the table go still—a wooden box the color of aged whiskey, its surface carved with Celtic knots that had been worn smooth by generations of fingers tracing their endless paths.

"Now?" Duncan asked, straightening in his chair. "You're doing this now?"

"Your grandfather left specific instructions," Mick said from his throne at the table's head, his blue eyes carrying that special gleam that meant tradition was about to assert itself. "This was to be given to Aidan on his thirty-fifth birthday."

"Which was last week," Hank pointed out.

Aidan stared at the box, his frustration about Dylan and the mysterious Seattle man temporarily forgotten. His grandfather's treasure box—the one that had sat on the mantle like a guardian of secrets, unopened since Patrick O'Hara's death three years ago.

"Whatever's in there," he said slowly, "it's going to complicate my life, isn't it?"

"When has anything from Grandda ever been simple?" Wyatt asked with the wisdom of the youngest son.

Anne set the box before Aidan with the ceremony it deserved. "Open it."

Inside, nestled on velvet the color of old wine, lay a claddagh ring. The silver caught the light like captured moonbeams, its surface polished, though well worn—two hands holding a crowned heart, the ancient symbol of love, loyalty, and friendship that had traveled from Ireland with the first O'Hara to seek his fortune in America.

"This ring," Mick began, his voice taking on the cadence of inherited memory, "has been in our family for three hundred years. It came across during the famine years, survived everything

America could throw at an Irish family, and now it comes to you—the last unmarried O'Hara son."

"I'm perfectly happy being unmarried," Aidan said, though even to his own ears it sounded hollow. Especially with the image of Dylan listening intently to whatever that Seattle man was selling burning in his mind.

"Are you?" Anne asked gently.

"There's more," Mick said, gesturing to the box.

Beneath the velvet was an envelope, sealed with wax the color of dried blood. Written across the front in their grandfather's distinctive scrawl— *To be opened only by the final bachelor O'Hara.*

Aidan broke the seal and unfolded the letter, his grandfather's words rising from the page like smoke from a peat fire.

"'My dear boy—and I know it's you, Aidan. You got my looks and my charm, which means you've got my weakness too. You think life's a dance where you never have to pick a partner for more than one song.

"'By now, they've shown you the ring. It's a fine ring, and it's served the family well. But here's the truth of it, boy—that's not the real ring.'"

There was a collective gasp around the table, and they all started talking at once. But Mick just raised his hand and everyone quieted back down.

Aidan continued. "'The real claddagh ring, the one blessed by a priest in Galway before the hunger took half of Ireland, is hidden. I've left it somewhere on this land, along with clues to find it. Why? Because nothing worth having comes easy, and love least of all.

"'You want to know the secret of the O'Haras? It's not charm or looks or the gift of the gab. It's knowing how to work for something. How to earn it. Your grandmother made me prove myself seven times before she'd be my wife.

"'So here's your first clue—Where iron horses once ran free, / before the mountain came to be, / Where settlers first put down their claim, / before O'Hara was our name.

"'Find the ring, boy. But more than that, find someone worth giving it to. Someone who'll make you want to stop dancing and finally learn to stand still.

"'With love and a gentle push, Patrick Michael O'Hara.

"'PS. Don't let your brothers help. They mean well, but this is your adventure. Find someone clever, with brains and heart. And for the love of all that's holy, find someone who can't be charmed by that smile of yours.'"

The room erupted in overlapping voices, but Aidan's mind had already gone to one person. Dylan. She could solve any puzzle, had a mind that worked in ways that constantly surprised him, and she was absolutely, completely immune to his charm. If anything, she seemed to find him vaguely annoying most days.

"Iron horses—that's trains," Raven was saying.

"The old railroad bed runs through the property," Wyatt added.

But Aidan was thinking about Dylan, about the way she'd looked that morning working on the Barracuda, completely absorbed in bringing something beautiful back to life. About how she'd promised to come to book club Thursday but probably wouldn't. About how some businessman from Seattle was trying to steal her away when Aidan had only just realized—

Realized what? That he'd been watching her for years without really seeing her? That her careful distance had become a challenge he wanted to overcome? That the thought of her leaving Laurel Valley made his chest tight with something that felt dangerously close to panic?

"You know who's clever," Sophie said with studied innocence. "Dylan Flanagan. She's got the kind of mind that could solve your grandfather's riddles."

"If she's not too busy considering job offers from Seattle," Raven added, and Aidan didn't miss the look that passed between his sisters-in-law.

"Job offers?" Aidan's voice was sharper than intended.

"That's what Shannon thought," Sophie said. "All those documents he was showing her? Looked very official. Very lucrative. The kind of opportunity that could change someone's life."

The thought made something fierce and possessive rise in Aidan's chest—a feeling he'd never experienced before, not with any of the women he'd dated over the years. Those relationships had been easy, comfortable, ultimately disposable. But Dylan…

Dylan was different. Had always been different. He just hadn't let himself see it until now.

"I'll figure out the clues myself," he said, pocketing the letter.

"Sure you will," Duncan said with elder-brother skepticism. "Just like you figured out how to do your own taxes."

"That was different—"

"Or how to bake a cake for Mom's birthday—"

"Okay, okay." Aidan held up his hands in surrender. "Maybe I could use some help. Someone who thinks differently than me."

"Someone clever," Sophie said, her smile innocent as spring rain.

"Someone who can't be charmed," Raven added.

"Someone who might already be making plans to leave town if you don't move fast," Anne said quietly, and her words carried the weight of maternal wisdom that couldn't be ignored.

Aidan looked around the table at his family—his brothers who'd all found their perfect matches, his parents who'd been together forty years, the children who represented the next generation of O'Haras who would call Laurel Valley home.

Then he thought about Dylan, alone in her apartment above the antique shop, probably reading one of those mysteries Sophie saved for her, definitely not thinking about him at all.

"I'll ask her," he said finally. "Tomorrow. If she hasn't already decided to take whatever that suit was selling."

"His name is Marcus Rowan," Sophie supplied helpfully. "He's staying at Laurel Valley B&B until tomorrow and Lorraine told me about him when she came in to buy some coffee table books. He owns Pacific Custom Restoration."

"Yeah, I recognize the name," Aidan said through gritted teeth.

"Well, we don't know the name," Duncan said, arching a brow. "Who is he?"

"Businessman," Sophie said. "Owns restoration garages through the Pacific Northwest all the way down the coast into California. He's very successful. Very persistent. According to Lorraine, that's who Jay Leno uses to restore all his cars."

The fork in Aidan's hand bent slightly.

"Easy there," Hank said, grinning. "Mom's good silverware doesn't deserve whatever you're imagining doing to Marcus Rowan."

As the evening wound down and the family dispersed into the October night, Aidan stood on the porch looking out at the land that had been in his family for five generations. Somewhere out there, his grandfather had hidden a ring that represented everything the O'Haras stood for— love, loyalty, friendship, tradition.

But first, he had to convince Dylan to help him find it.

And maybe, if he was very lucky and considerably less charming than usual, he could convince her that whatever Seattle was offering wasn't worth leaving Laurel Valley.

That staying—staying for the town, for the garage, maybe even for him—was worth considering.

The thought terrified him more than any challenge his grandfather could have devised.

Which probably meant it was exactly what he needed.

Chapter Three

Monday morning arrived with the kind of pristine clarity that made the mountains look like they'd been cut from glass and placed against a painted sky. Dylan had spent the weekend in self-imposed exile, walking the trails above town where she could think without the weight of watching eyes, turning Marcus Rowan's offer over in her mind like a restoration project she couldn't quite figure out how to approach.

Ten thousand dollars. A restoration bay of her own. The chance to work on cars that belonged in museums—Duesenbergs and Bugattis, the kind of automobiles that were art as much as engineering. It should have been an easy decision. Would have been, for someone who hadn't spent five years accidentally growing roots in a place she'd only meant to pass through.

The Pinnacle Garage welcomed her at six with its familiar embrace of motor oil and possibility. She'd beaten everyone there, as always, needing the quiet hour before the day began its demands. The Ferrari sat in her bay like a satisfied cat, its fuel injection problem solved, waiting for its owner to remember where he'd left it. Three days it had been sitting there, three days at five hundred dollars a day in storage fees that the owner would pay without blinking. Rich people, she'd learned, had different relationships with their possessions—they could afford to forget about things worth more than most people's houses.

Dylan made coffee in the ancient machine, the ritual as necessary as breathing. Black, no sugar, no complications—the same way she'd been drinking it since her father had let her have her first cup at fourteen, working beside him in a garage not so different from this one. Through the windows, she watched Laurel Valley wake up— delivery trucks making their rounds, Rose arranging pastries in the bakery window that would sell out by noon, the town preparing its daily performance of quaint mountain charm for the tourists who'd start arriving by nine.

The morning light had an autumn quality, honey thick and generous, transforming everything it touched into something worth remembering. It painted the mountains in shades of amber and gold, turned the shop windows into mirrors of flame, made even the practical lines of the garage seem softer, more forgiving.

Her phone sat silent on the workbench. Marcus had texted twice over the weekend, professionally persistent without crossing into pushy. Today he needed an answer. Today she had to choose between the practical decision and the impractical life she'd somehow built here.

She thought about Patrick O'Hara. Aidan's grandfather had been one of the first people to make her feel welcome in Laurel Valley, stopping by the garage in those early days when she was still learning everyone's names and their cars' peculiarities. He'd had that Irish gift for making you feel like you were the most interesting person in the room, even when you were just a stranger covered in motor oil.

"You've got healing hands," he'd told her once, watching her work on a 1965 Mustang.

"Not everyone can bring dead things back to life. That's a gift, that is. A kind of magic."

She'd thought he was just being kind, the way old men sometimes were, full of blarney and compliments that cost nothing to give. But there'd been something in his eyes—a recognition, maybe, of one outsider to another. He'd been gone three years now, but she still sometimes expected to see him walking through the door with that rolling gait and that smile that made you believe in possibilities.

She was underneath a Bentley, addressing a minor exhaust issue that the owner insisted was "catastrophic," when she heard the door open. Not Ralph's cheerful entrance that always announced itself with off-key humming, or Danny's exhausted shuffle accompanied by the scent of baby formula. These footsteps carried purpose, moving through the garage with the determination of someone who'd spent the weekend building up to something.

"Morning, Dylan."

Aidan's voice made her grip tighten on the wrench. She'd managed to avoid thinking about him for almost ten whole minutes—a personal record for the weekend.

"Morning," she called back, not emerging from under the Bentley, not ready to face those green eyes that had haunted her all weekend, mixing unhelpfully with thoughts of escape routes and signing bonuses.

She heard him move closer, could feel him standing just outside her peripheral vision. The silence stretched between them, unusual for Aidan who typically filled every space with easy conversation about weekend plans or the weather or whatever project was currently driving him to distraction.

"Busy weekend?" he finally asked, and something in his tone made her slide out from under the car.

He was leaning against her tool chest, aiming for casual but missing by miles. His jaw was tight, his hands shoved deep in his pockets, and he was looking at her with an intensity that made her stomach perform a complicated maneuver that definitely wasn't in any anatomy textbook.

Dylan sat up on the creeper, wiping her hands on a shop rag with meticulous care. "Quiet," she said. "You?"

"Family dinner yesterday. The usual chaos." He paused, and she could see him choosing his words like he was selecting tools for a delicate repair. "Sophie mentioned she saw you having lunch at The Lampstand on Friday."

There it was. Dylan turned her attention to the rag in her hands, cleaning grease from beneath her nails with focused precision. "I did."

"With Marcus Rowan."

"You know him?"

"I know of him. Pacific Custom Restoration has a reputation for excellence." The words came out neutral, but she could hear the effort it took, like watching someone lift an engine block and pretend it weighed nothing. "He trying to poach you?"

Dylan stood slowly, meeting his eyes directly because she'd learned long ago that difficult conversations were best faced head-on. "He made me an offer."

Something flickered across Aidan's face—surprise, certainly, but underneath it something else. Something that looked almost like hurt. "Are you considering it?"

"I'd be foolish not to." She kept her voice level, professional, the same tone she used when explaining to customers why their repairs would cost more than expected. "It's a good opportunity."

"Right. Of course." He nodded, but his knuckles had gone white where he gripped the edge of the tool chest. "When do you have to decide?"

"Today."

The word hung between them like suspended exhaust, toxic and impossible to ignore. Aidan pushed off from the tool chest, pacing a few steps before turning back to her. His usual easy confidence had been replaced with something more raw, more real, and it made him paradoxically more attractive than any of his practiced charm ever had.

"I need to ask you something," he said, pulling a folded paper from his pocket. "A favor. And I know the timing is terrible, and you've got this big decision to make, but…"

He trailed off, running his hand through his hair in a gesture she'd seen a thousand times when he was frustrated with a stubborn bolt or a diagnosis that didn't make sense. But she'd never seen him frustrated with words before. Aidan O'Hara always knew what to say.

"What kind of favor?" Dylan asked, curiosity overriding caution.

"My grandfather left me something. Instructions, really. A treasure hunt." He unfolded the paper, handling it with unexpected reverence. "You remember my grandfather."

It wasn't a question. Patrick O'Hara wasn't someone you forgot.

"He used to bring me butterscotch candies," Dylan said softly, surprising herself with the memory. "Said they were for customers, but he always made sure I got one."

Aidan's face softened. "He liked you. Said you had an old soul and young hands, whatever that meant."

"It meant I could understand old cars but still had steady enough hands to fix them." Dylan found herself smiling despite everything. "He had a way with words."

"He had a way with everything. Including making things complicated." Aidan held out the paper. "He hid something—a family heirloom. Left clues to find it. His letter said I'd need help from someone clever, someone who thinks differently than I do."

Dylan took the paper. The handwriting was distinctive—the precise script of someone who'd learned penmanship when it was still an art.

"'Where iron horses once ran free," she read aloud, "before the mountain came to be, / where settlers first put down their claim, / before O'Hara was our name.'"

Her mind immediately began working the puzzle, grateful for something concrete to focus on while her heart attempted to maintain something like normal rhythm. "Iron horses—that's trains. The old railroad line that ran through the valley."

"That's what my family figured, but it's miles of track bed. We need to narrow it down somehow."

"The second part is key," she murmured, studying the words with the same intensity she brought to diagnostic problems. "Before the mountain came to be—that's not literal. Mountains don't just appear. Maybe it means before something was named? Or before development? Was there a time when part of your land wasn't called a mountain?"

"I have no idea." Aidan moved closer, ostensibly to look at the paper, but she could feel the heat of him, could smell that pine soap that had been undermining her concentration for five years. "My grandfather loved his puzzles, but he always said they had logical answers if you knew how to look. He said the same thing about engines, actually. That every problem had a solution if you could see past what you expected to find."

"Wise man," Dylan said, handing back the paper before she did something stupid like lean into Aidan's warmth.

"He was." Aidan refolded the letter with precision. "Would you help me? I know you've got this big decision to make, and if you take the Seattle job—"

"It's not in Seattle," she corrected automatically. "The shop is. But Marcus said I could work out of any of their locations. They have one in Bozeman."

Aidan went very still. "Bozeman's only three hours away."

"Two and a half if you don't hit traffic."

"That's…that's not leaving. That's commuting distance."

Dylan hadn't thought of it that way, but he was right. She could keep her apartment, still come back to Laurel Valley on weekends. It was a compromise she hadn't let herself fully consider.

"Would you help me?" Aidan asked, his tone shifting to something more businesslike. "Saturday morning. We could start at the old railroad bed, work through the clues systematically. I'll bring coffee and those apple cider donuts from Heavenly Delights."

"You remember my donut preference?" Dylan was surprised he'd noticed.

"I notice more than you think." There was something in the way he said it that made her pulse skip. "Eight o'clock? We can meet at the Pine Ridge turnout."

It wasn't really a question—he was already assuming she'd say yes. The confidence should have annoyed her, but instead she found it oddly appealing. This was the Aidan who ran a successful business, who made decisions and followed through.

"Fine," she said, trying to sound more reluctant than she felt. "But I'm only doing this because I respected your grandfather."

"Of course," Aidan agreed, though his slight smile suggested he wasn't buying it entirely. "Patrick would appreciate you helping carry on his unique brand of torture."

"He'd probably find the whole thing hilarious," Dylan said, remembering the old man's wicked sense of humor.

"He would." Aidan's expression softened. "He always said the best treasures were the ones you had to work for. I'm starting to think he wasn't just talking about the ring."

She should say no. Should maintain the distance that had kept her heart relatively intact for five years. Should make her decision about Marcus Rowan's offer based on logic and financial sense, not on the way Aidan O'Hara's eyes lit up when he talked about his grandfather.

"Patrick would have loved this," she said instead of answering directly. "A treasure hunt, making you work for something. He always said the O'Hara boys had everything too easy."

"He wasn't wrong." Aidan's smile was rueful and oddly charming in its self-awareness. "Everything except figuring out what actually matters."

Before Dylan could parse what that meant, the door burst open and Ralph's voice filled the garage like sunshine after rain.

"Morning, everyone! Another beautiful day in paradise!" He stopped short, taking in the scene—Dylan and Aidan standing closer than professional distance dictated, both of them looking like they'd been caught at something. "Am I interrupting?"

"No," Dylan said quickly, stepping back and grabbing a wrench she didn't need. "Just discussing Saturday."

"Saturday?" Ralph's mustache twitched with interest. "What's happening Saturday?"

"Dylan's helping me with a project," Aidan said smoothly, his professional mask sliding back into place. "Family thing."

"Family thing," Ralph repeated, his tone suggesting he wasn't buying it for a second. "Well, don't let me interrupt your…family thing discussion."

Aidan headed toward his office, leaving Dylan to face Ralph's knowing grin alone.

"Not a word," she warned.

"Wouldn't dream of it," Ralph said cheerfully, then immediately launched into an operatic rendition of "Some Enchanted Evening" that followed her all the way back under the Bentley.

But as Dylan returned to work, her mind kept circling back to the puzzle. Where iron horses once ran free. Before the mountain came to be. There was something familiar about the phrasing, something that tickled the edge of memory like a word you couldn't quite recall.

She thought about Patrick O'Hara, about the way he'd told stories that made you lean in despite yourself. He'd talked about the old days some-times, about how Laurel Valley had changed, how the railroad had brought prosperity and then abandonment in equal measure. There'd been a story about a mountain that wasn't a mountain, about a hill that had been renamed when the ski resort developers arrived, seeing profit in what had once been just another piece of the landscape.

O'Hara's Peak. That's what they called it now, the ski runs that brought thousands of tourists every winter. But Patrick had called it something else once, when he'd been telling her about the early days. What was it?

Her phone buzzed. Marcus Rowan, politely requesting a decision.

Dylan looked at the text, then at the garage around her—Ralph now singing to his tools, Danny arriving with new pictures of his daughter, the familiar rhythm of a Monday morning at The Pinnacle. Through the window, she could see Aidan in his office, frowning at paperwork with the same concentration he brought to everything that mattered to him.

She thought about Patrick O'Hara's treasure hunt, about family heirlooms and hidden rings and the way Aidan had said "everything except figuring out what actually matters."

Maybe that's what this was really about. Not just finding a ring, but finding what mattered. And maybe, just maybe, helping Aidan search for his grandfather's treasure would help her find her own answer about whether to stay or go.

Dylan typed a response to Marcus: *I appreciate your offer and your patience. I need until next Monday to give you a proper answer. This is my home, and leaving isn't a decision I take lightly.*

His response came quickly: *Of course. Take the time you need. Good mechanics are worth waiting for, but great ones—the kind who can make a '70 Barracuda sing—they're worth whatever time they need.*

Dylan smiled at the screen. He'd done his homework, knew about the Barracuda. That was either impressive or slightly unsettling, but either way, it reminded her that she had something valuable to offer. She wasn't just another mechanic looking for a better paycheck. She was an artist, and her work had caught the attention of someone who recognized its worth.

She tucked her phone away and got back to work on the Bentley, her mind already turning over Patrick's riddle. Where iron horses once ran free. There was an answer there, waiting to be discovered, just like there was an answer to her own puzzle about staying or leaving.

Saturday couldn't come fast enough. Not because she was eager to spend time with Aidan —well, not just because of that—but because maybe, in helping him find what his grandfather had hidden, she'd finally figure out what she'd been searching for all along.

Chapter Four

Saturday morning arrived dressed in fog, the mountains invisible behind veils of white that turned Laurel Valley into something from a fairy tale—mysterious, ethereal, holding its breath for what might happen next. Dylan reached the Pine Ridge turnout at seven forty-five, fifteen minutes early because she'd been awake since four, her mind refusing to quiet its endless circling around riddles and rings and the dangerous territory of hope.

She'd spent the week diving into research during her lunch breaks, haunting the historical society's archives like a woman possessed. Mrs. Whitfield, the elderly librarian who guarded the archives with the ferocity of a dragon protecting gold, had eventually warmed to her quest, pulling out documents that hadn't seen daylight in decades.

"The O'Haras," Mrs. Whitfield had said, her voice carrying the reverence reserved for founding families, "came here when there was nothing but wilderness and possibility. Two brothers from County Sligo, following stories of land that looked like home."

The documents told a story Dylan had only heard fragments of—how those two O'Hara brothers had arrived in 1847, when Idaho was still untamed territory, when Laurel Valley was nothing but a dream waiting to be named. They'd claimed land that reminded them of Ireland, with its own mountain and lake, its own harsh beauty that could break your heart or make your fortune depending on how you approached it.

Standing now in the fog-wrapped morning, waiting for Aidan, Dylan thought about those first O'Haras. What kind of courage did it take to leave everything behind, to stake your claim on land that didn't even have proper maps yet? They'd built their first shelter with their own hands, turned wilderness into ranch land, raised families who would become the backbone of a town that didn't exist yet.

The irony wasn't lost on her—here she was, afraid to commit to a place that had been civilized for over a century, while the O'Haras had committed to raw land with nothing but hope and determination.

Thursday night had come and gone without her attending the book club. Sophie had texted her twice—once to remind her, once to ask if she was okay—and Dylan had stared at those messages with the guilt of someone who'd forgotten something that mattered. But how could she explain that she'd been so lost in thoughts of treasure hunts and job offers that she'd forgotten about the one social commitment she'd actually made?

The truth sat heavy in her chest: Marcus Rowan's offer wasn't really the issue. What she wanted—what she'd always wanted since she'd started turning wrenches beside her father—was her own shop. A place where she could take her time, where every restoration could be art instead of just repair. But that dream required money she didn't have, credit she couldn't get, and a faith in permanence she'd never learned to cultivate.

Aidan's truck materialized through the fog at exactly eight o'clock, its headlights cutting through the white like lighthouse beams guiding ships to safety. He parked beside her Charger, and through the mist-softened glass, she watched him check his reflection in the mirror, smoothing his hair in a gesture so unconsciously vain and oddly vulnerable that her heart performed a complicated maneuver in her chest.

"Morning," he called, climbing out with a thermos and bakery bag that released the scent of cinnamon and possibility into the cool morning air. "I brought reinforcements."

"Rose's apple cider donuts?"

"As promised. Still warm. I may have charmed Rose into making a fresh batch just for us."

"Of course you did." But there was no bite to it. This was Aidan's gift—making people want to do things for him, not through manipulation but through genuine warmth that made you feel like you were part of something special just by being near him.

They stood for a moment in the swirling fog, neither quite sure how to navigate this new territory—choosing to spend time together outside the familiar boundaries of work, outside the safe roles of boss and employee.

"I did some research," Dylan said, needing something concrete to anchor herself. "About your family's history, the railroad, all of it. Mrs. Whitfield at the historical society was very helpful."

"You went to see Mrs. Whitfield?" Aidan's eyebrows rose. "She usually guards those archives like they contain state secrets."

"She warmed up when I told her I was trying to solve one of Patrick O'Hara's riddles. Apparently, she had quite the crush on him when she was younger."

Aidan's laugh was warm and genuine. "Grandda had that effect on women. Even in his eighties, he could charm the paint off a barn."

"He was kind," Dylan said simply. "That's rarer than charm."

They climbed into Aidan's truck—her suggestion, practical given the rough roads ahead—and she tried not to notice how the cab smelled like him, pine and possibility. As they drove, Aidan told her stories she'd never heard, filling in the gaps between historical records and lived memory.

"The two brothers who came here first," he said, navigating the forest road with practiced ease, "were Thomas and Seamus. They'd lost everything in Ireland—the British took their land after some uprising, and they figured they had nothing left to lose by starting over."

"The Nine Years' War," Dylan said, surprising him. "Mrs. Whitfield had records. Your family fought with pitchforks and axes against British soldiers with guns and armor."

"You really did research."

"I like understanding how things connect." She watched the forest pass outside the window, trees emerging and disappearing in the fog like ghosts. "They named this place Laurel Valley, but before that, before the Bavarian settlers came and built their perfect little Alpine village, this was just O'Hara land."

"Still is, mostly," Aidan said with a pride that went bone deep. "We've sold some over the years, developed other parts, but the core of it—the ranch, the mountain, the lakes—that's still ours."

"That's what I don't understand," Dylan admitted. "How do you stay? How do you look at the same views every day, walk the same paths, and not feel trapped?"

Aidan was quiet for a moment, considering. "I guess I don't see the same views. Every season changes them. Every sunrise is different. And the paths…" He glanced at her, something soft in his expression. "The paths lead to different places depending on who you're walking them with."

The weight of that observation settled between them, too heavy for the fragile peace they'd established. Dylan turned back to the window, watching as they climbed higher into the mountains, leaving the fog behind for crystalline morning light that turned everything to gold.

The homestead ruins appeared through the trees like something from a dream—stone foundations overtaken by moss, wooden beams collapsed into abstract sculptures of decay. This wasn't the grand ranch house where Aidan had grown up—that stood miles away, built by his father's hands as his family grew. This was the original, the first shelter those O'Hara brothers had built in 1847 when Idaho was still wild and unforgiving.

"This is where it all started," Aidan said, his voice carrying the reverence of someone standing on holy ground.

They walked through the ruins together, and Dylan found herself seeing it not as abandoned stones but as the beginning of something that had endured for nearly two centuries. Here, Thomas or Seamus had laid the first foundation stone. Here, their wives had cooked over open fires, their children had taken first steps, their dreams had either flourished or withered depending on the harshness of winter and the generosity of summer.

"The railroad came through in the 1880s," Dylan said, orienting herself with the mental map she'd constructed from old documents. "By then, your family had already been here for thirty years. They'd already named the mountain, claimed the water rights, established themselves as the ones who stayed when others gave up."

"Before the mountain came to be," Aidan murmured, understanding dawning. "Not before the literal mountain existed, but before it had a name. Before it became O'Hara's Peak."

"And before O'Hara was our name," Dylan continued. "Mrs. Whitfield showed me immigration records. The family name was originally Ó hEaghra. It got Americanized at some point, probably when the government started requiring official documentation."

They searched methodically through the ruins, Dylan applying the same systematic approach she used for diagnostics. If Patrick had hidden something here, it would be somewhere significant but protected. The morning sun climbed higher, burning off the last of the fog, revealing the valley spread below them like a map of possibilities.

"Here," she called from the far corner of the foundation. "This stone is different."

Aidan crouched beside her, their shoulders touching as they examined what she'd found. The stone was newer than the others, the mortar less weathered. Someone—Patrick, presumably—had removed and replaced it, creating a hiding spot that would survive weather and time.

Together, they worked it free, revealing a metal box wrapped in oilcloth. Inside, Patrick's handwriting waited for them, patient as memory:

Where water speaks but never flows, / where secrets rest that no one knows.

"Water that speaks," Dylan mused, sitting back on her heels, her mind already working through possibilities.

"There are dozens of water sources on the property," Aidan said, frustration creeping into his voice. "Springs, streams, two lakes, the old irrigation channels from when this was all cattle land."

"But this is specifically water that speaks but doesn't flow." Dylan stood, brushing dirt from her jeans. "That's unusual. Most water either moves or it's silent."

"Unless..." Aidan's eyes lit up. "The well. There's an old well on the back forty. We used to drop stones down it as kids, listening to the echo.

Water that speaks when something disturbs it, but it doesn't flow anywhere."

"How far is it?"

"From here? Maybe three miles through the forest, or we can go back and drive around the long way."

Dylan looked at the sun climbing through the trees, calculating time and distance. "Let's walk. I want to see more of the land."

They set off through the forest, following a trail that might have been made by deer or might have been worn by generations of O'Hara children playing in their backyard wilderness. Aidan moved with the confidence of someone who'd memorized every tree, every stone, every shift in elevation. Dylan found herself watching him as much as the path, seeing him in his element in a way the garage never quite allowed.

"Tell me about your grandfather," she said as they walked. "The real him, not just the stories everyone tells."

Aidan ducked under a low branch, holding it aside for her. "He was complicated. Everyone remembers the charming Irishman with a story for every occasion, but there was more to him than that. He'd seen things in Korea that he never talked about. Lost friends. Came home different, my grandmother said."

"Is that why he liked puzzles? To keep his mind busy?"

"Maybe. Or maybe he just liked making us work for things. He always said the O'Haras had it too easy, that struggle built character."

They emerged into a clearing where the remains of an old cabin stood, barely more than a chimney and a few foundation stones. Aidan stopped, his expression shifting to something Dylan couldn't read.

"This was where my great-great-uncle lived," he said quietly. "Seamus's son. He was what they called 'simple' back then. Couldn't handle town, couldn't handle people, but he could gentle any horse, grow anything in soil everyone else said was worthless. The family built him this cabin so he could live on his own terms."

"They took care of him," Dylan said, understanding. "Even when it would have been easier to send him away."

"O'Haras don't abandon their own." The words carried weight, like a vow passed down through generations. "It's why the family's survived everything—the Nine Years' War, the famine, the journey to America, the Depression, droughts, fires. We stay together."

Something in Dylan's chest ached at that—the promise of belonging she'd never had, the security of knowing that no matter what, someone would catch you if you fell. Her own family had scattered like dandelion seeds after her father's death, each carrying their grief in different directions.

They continued walking, the forest growing denser, older, until they reached another clearing where a stone circle marked the location of the old well. Someone—probably Aidan's father— had covered it with heavy planks years ago, a safety measure for a new generation of adventurous children.

"Water that speaks," Dylan said softly as they pried off the boards.

When they dropped a stone into the darkness, the echo that came back was like a voice from the past—hollow, patient, keeping secrets in the dark. They searched the well's rim, Dylan's fingers finding the subtle differences in mortar that suggested Patrick's handiwork.

"Here," she said, pressing on a stone that gave slightly under pressure.

It took both of them to work it free, revealing another oilcloth bundle, another piece of the puzzle. But when Dylan unfolded the paper, she found not just a clue but a longer message in Patrick's script:

"'Well done, boy. If you're reading this, then you've brought the clever one with you, the one who sees patterns where others see chaos. Your grandmother was like that—could look at a field and see the garden it could become, look at a young man full of anger from war and see the husband he might be.

"'The ring is closer now, but first another truth—the O'Haras didn't survive by strength alone. We survived because we knew when to fight and when to build, when to stand firm and when to bend. We survived because we found partners who made us better than we were alone.

"'Your next clue—Where love first bloomed on O'Hara land, / where promises were made by heart and hand, / look for the place where two became one, / beneath the tree that faces the sun.'"

Dylan's hands trembled slightly as she finished reading. "He's not just sending you on a treasure hunt."

"No," Aidan agreed, his voice rough. "He's trying to teach me something."

"About what?"

"About what actually matters. About the difference between existing and living. About... About how the O'Haras really survived all these years."

They stood there in the clearing, the weight of history and expectation settling around them like fog. Somewhere in these mountains was a ring that had crossed an ocean, survived famines and wars, been worn by men and women who'd built something from nothing. But Patrick hadn't hidden it just to make Aidan work for it.

He'd hidden it to make him understand what it meant.

"Where did your grandparents get married?" Dylan asked, practical even in the face of revelation.

"In town, at the church. But that's not where he proposed." Aidan's eyes went distant, remembering. "There's a tree by the east lake. An oak that's older than anything else on the property. He told me once that's where he asked her, where she said yes."

"How far?"

"From here? Another two miles, maybe three."

Dylan looked at the sun, now high overhead. They'd been walking for hours, piecing together not just clues but the entire story of a family that had endured against all odds. Her legs were tired, her mind was spinning, but something in her wanted to keep going, to see how this story played out.

"We should come back next week," she said instead, the practical part of her asserting itself. "Plan better, bring supplies."

Aidan looked like he wanted to protest, then nodded. "You're right. Besides, Grandda waited three years to give me this puzzle. He'd probably approve of making me wait a little longer."

As they walked back toward the truck, taking a different path that Aidan promised was shorter, Dylan found herself thinking about permanence, about roots, about what it meant to stay. The O'Haras had been here since before Laurel Valley existed. They'd shaped the land and been shaped by it in return. They'd built something that lasted not through stubbornness alone but through adaptation, through choosing the right partners, through knowing when to hold tight and when to let go.

"Can I ask you something?" Aidan said as

they emerged from the forest onto the road where they'd left his truck.

"Depends on the question."

"Why didn't you come to book club Thursday?"

The question caught her off guard, too direct for the cautious dance they'd been doing all morning. "I forgot," she admitted. "I've been distracted."

"By the job offer?"

"By everything." She stopped walking, needing to say this while she wasn't looking at him, while the words could float free without the weight of his green eyes. "The job isn't really the issue. Marcus could offer me twice as much and it wouldn't solve the real problem."

"Which is?"

"I want my own shop. My own place where I can do restorations the way they should be done. Where I can choose projects that matter, that bring something beautiful back to life." The words came out in a rush, a dream she'd never voiced aloud before. "But that takes money I don't have, credit I can't get, and faith that I could actually build something lasting."

She felt rather than saw Aidan go still beside her. When he spoke, his voice was careful, considered. "What if you could?"

"Could what?"

"Have your own shop. Here. In Laurel Valley."

Dylan turned to look at him, sure she'd misheard. "That's not—I just told you I don't have the money."

"But what if you did? What if there was a way?"

Something in his expression made her heart race—intensity and possibility and what looked dangerously like determination. "Aidan, what are you talking about?"

He seemed to catch himself, stepping back from whatever edge he'd been approaching. "Nothing. Just…thinking out loud. Forget I said anything."

But Dylan couldn't forget. As they drove back toward town, the silence between them comfortable despite the weight of unspoken possibilities, she kept turning his words over in her mind. What if she could? What if there was a way to have everything she wanted without having to leave?

The thought was dangerous. Hope was dangerous. Because once you started believing something was possible, you started making space for it in your life. And Dylan had learned long ago that the more space you made for dreams, the more it hurt when they didn't come true.

But sitting in Aidan's truck, watching him navigate roads his family had been traveling for almost two centuries, Dylan felt something shift inside her chest. Maybe it was the morning spent walking through history. Maybe it was Patrick's riddles working their own kind of magic. Or maybe it was just Aidan himself, solid and real beside her, making her believe that some things were worth the risk of wanting them.

"Same time next week?" he asked when they reached the turnout where her car waited.

"I'll be here," she promised, and meant it.

As she drove back toward town, following the curves of a road that had been carved through wilderness by men who believed in permanence, Dylan thought about roots and wings, about staying and leaving, about the courage it took to do either.

The O'Haras had come to this valley with nothing but determination and hope. They'd built

something that lasted, something worth protecting, something worth passing on.

Maybe it was time for Dylan Flanagan to stop
running long enough to see if she could build
something too.

Chapter Five

SUNDAY MORNING DESCENDED ON LAUREL VALLEY dressed in church bells and sunshine, the kind of morning that made even skeptics consider the possibility of grace. Dylan stood at her apartment window, coffee cooling in her hands, watching families make their way toward the white-steepled church at the center of town. The O'Haras would be among them—five brothers in their Sunday best, wives corralling children, Anne and Mick leading the procession like they'd been doing for forty years.

Tomorrow, Marcus Rowan needed an answer. Tomorrow, she had to choose between the practical path and the impractical life she'd been building here one day at a time.

But today, she had paint on her hands and a half-transformed apartment that suddenly felt too small for all the feelings she'd been trying to contain since yesterday's treasure hunt.

The apartment above Millicent's Antiques had always been temporary in her mind—a place to sleep, to store her few possessions, to exist between workdays. She'd never hung pictures, never bought curtains to replace the yellowed ones that had come with the place, never done anything that might suggest permanence. But yesterday, walking through ruins that had sheltered the first O'Haras in 1847, something had shifted.

Dylan dipped her roller in the paint tray, watching the warm terra-cotta color cling to the foam. The first wall had been an accident—she'd bought the paint on impulse Friday night, driven by a restlessness she couldn't name. But now, Sunday afternoon, with three walls done and her furniture pushed to the center of the room like islands in a sea of drop cloths, she understood what she was doing.

She was nesting. Building. Making space for a life that might actually happen instead of one she was just passing through.

Church bells rang again, signaling the end of service. In an hour, the O'Haras would gather at their farmhouse for Sunday dinner, the table groaning under Anne's cooking, the house filled with the chaos of family. Dylan had heard Sophie describe it with the reverence usually reserved for sacred rituals.

Her phone buzzed. A text from Aidan: *Found something about the well in my grandmother's diary. Want to see?*

Her heart did that stupid skip it had been perfecting since yesterday. She stared at the message, thumb hovering over the keyboard. The smart thing would be to wait until Saturday. Keep the boundaries clear. Maintain the fiction that this was just about helping with his grandfather's puzzle.

She typed: *When?*

After dinner? Around 3? Everyone will be in food comas by then.

Three o'clock. After church, after Sunday dinner, when the family would be scattered between naps and football. A safer time than joining them for the meal itself.

I'll be there, she sent before she could think better of it.

Dylan returned to her painting, but her mind

kept circling back to yesterday. The way Aidan had moved through his family's history with such reverence. The way he'd looked at her when she'd solved the first part of the riddle. The way Patrick's clue had felt like more than just directions to a hiding place.

By the time three o'clock approached, she'd finished the last wall and stood in the center of her transformed space. The warm terra-cotta made the room glow even in afternoon shadow, made it feel like somewhere a person might actually live rather than just exist.

The drive to the O'Hara ranch took her through quiet Sunday streets. Most of Laurel Valley observed the Sabbath in some form—shops closed, families gathered, a collective pause in the week's rhythm. Even the tourists seemed subdued, as if the town's reverence was contagious.

The O'Hara house sprawled across its hilltop, the gray stone and white paint gleaming in afternoon sun. The white fences lined the paddocks where horses grazed, and the barns with their dark green roofs looked like something from a painting—*Rural Paradise*, oil on canvas.

She parked behind Aidan's truck, noting the collection of vehicles that suggested the full clan was still present. Through the windows, she could see movement—someone washing dishes, children running past, the comfortable chaos of family in its natural habitat.

The kitchen door opened before she could knock. Aidan stood there in jeans and a button-down shirt that suggested he'd changed after church but hadn't quite made it to completely casual.

"Good timing," he said. "I just escaped dish duty."

"How'd you manage that?"

"Told Mom I had important research to do for Grandda's treasure hunt. She's a sucker for anything involving family history."

He led her through the kitchen where Anne and Sophie were putting away leftovers, both women greeting her warmly but not stopping their conversation about Wednesday's church social and who was bringing what.

The hallway to Mick's office was lined with photographs—decades of O'Hara history captured in frames. Weddings and christenings, first days of school and championship rodeos, the visual DNA of a family that had stayed long enough to document its evolution.

"Dad's in the living room yelling at the Broncos," Aidan said, opening the office door. "We should have at least an hour before he remembers this is his sanctuary."

The office was exactly what Dylan would have expected from Mick O'Hara—masculine but warm, organized but lived in. The massive walnut desk dominated the space, and Aidan had spread papers across it like he was conducting an archaeological dig.

"Your grandmother's diary," Dylan said, spotting the leather-bound journal.

"She wrote about everything. The weather, the ranch, the boys. And Patrick." Aidan's voice softened on his grandfather's name. "She wrote about their courtship, their marriage, their life together. It's like having a window into who they really were, not just the stories everyone tells."

He opened the diary to a marked page, his grandmother's precise script filling the yellowed paper.

"'Patrick showed me the old well today,'" he read aloud. "'He says his grandfather used it to water the first garden they planted, that the water has special properties that make things grow. He made me drop a penny and make a wish. I wished he would kiss me. He did.'"

Dylan felt heat climb her neck. "That's… personal."

"There's more. Listen to this part. 'Patrick says the well keeps secrets better than any lock-box. That what goes down into that darkness stays there until someone knows the right way to call it back up.'"

"She knew," Dylan breathed. "Even then, she knew he was the type to hide things."

"Look at this." Aidan turned the page, pointing to an entry dated years later. "'Patrick and the boys spent all day at the old homestead. He's teaching them about their history, he says, but I know he's really teaching them about belonging. About staying. About being part of something bigger than themselves.'"

Dylan traced the words with her finger, careful not to damage the delicate paper. "He was preparing them even then. For this."

"For what, though? Just finding a ring?"

"For understanding what the ring means," Dylan said without thinking, then caught herself. "I mean, the family legacy and all that."

Aidan studied her with those green eyes that seemed to see more than she wanted to reveal. "Is that what you think this is about? Legacy?"

Before she could answer, the door burst open and Harrison skidded into the room, his church clothes replaced with play clothes that already showed evidence of outdoor adventures.

"Uncle Aidan! Mom says you have to come see! Chewy caught a snake and he won't let it go and Dad's afraid to grab it because what if it's poisonous and Uncle Colt says it's just a garden snake but Uncle Wyatt says we should call animal control and—"

"Breathe, buddy," Aidan said, already standing. "Where's Chewy now?"

"By the barn! Come on!"

Harrison grabbed Aidan's hand, then looked at Dylan with the consideration of a child deciding if someone was worth including.

"You should come too," he decided. "You might know about snakes."

"I really don't," Dylan said, but she was already following them out of the office, through the kitchen where Anne just shook her head with the patience of a woman who'd raised five boys, and out into the chaos of the backyard.

The entire O'Hara clan had gathered near the barn where Chewy, the enormous white dog, sat proudly with what was indeed a harmless garden snake writhing in his gentle mouth.

"Drop it," Duncan commanded with absolutely no effect.

"Chewy, release," Hank tried with similar results.

"This is ridiculous," Raven said, but she was laughing. "It's clearly not poisonous."

"All snakes look the same to me," Wyatt protested. "Dangerous."

"You're a cop," Colt pointed out. "You've faced armed criminals."

"Armed criminals don't slither. Want me to shoot it?"

Dylan found herself laughing at the absurdity of it—five grown men defeated by one dog and a garden snake. Without thinking, she walked over to Chewy, knelt down, and said quietly, "That's a good boy. Good hunter. Now give."

To everyone's amazement, Chewy immediately dropped the snake, which quickly disappeared into the tall grass.

"How did you do that?" Sophie asked.

"I have no idea," Dylan admitted. "My dad used to say I had a way with animals. Though we never had pets, so I'm not sure what he based that on."

"Maybe you're the dog whisperer," Harrison said solemnly. "Or the snake charmer!"

"Definitely the O'Hara charmer," Sophie said under her breath, but loud enough for Dylan to hear.

"All right, crisis averted," Anne announced. "Harrison, go wash your hands. Twice. With soap."

As the family dispersed, Aidan touched Dylan's elbow. "Want to see the barn? I have something to show you."

She followed him into the cool shadows of the barn, expecting horses but finding cars—a collection of vehicles in various states of restoration, including what looked like a 1969 Dodge Charger up on blocks.

"Is that—?"

"Same year as yours, different color. I bought it six months ago, thinking I'd restore it." He ran his hand along the dusty hood. "But I realized I don't have your touch. It needs someone who understands not just the mechanics but the soul of the machine."

Dylan moved closer, her trained eye cataloguing the work needed. "It's salvageable. Good bones."

"That's what I thought." Aidan leaned against a workbench, his expression turning serious. "Dylan, I need to talk to you about something. A business proposition."

Her stomach tightened. "Okay."

"The Pinnacle is doing well. Really well. We're booked solid for three months out, and I keep having to turn away restoration projects because we don't have the capacity or, honestly, the expertise for that level of work." He paused, choosing his words with care. "What if we expanded? Added a restoration division to The Pinnacle?"

"That would take significant investment—"

"Which I have. But more importantly, it would take someone with the skill to run it. Someone who understands the difference between repair and resurrection." His eyes held hers. "Someone like you."

Dylan's heart was racing. "What exactly are you proposing?"

"A partnership. You'd head the restoration division, build it from the ground up. You'd still work regular repairs when needed—we can't afford to lose you there—but as restoration projects came in, they'd be yours. You'd hire your own assistant when the time comes, set your own standards. Eventually, if it grows enough, it could be its own separate entity. But for now, it would be part of The Pinnacle."

"Why would you do this?"

"Because it's good business. There's demand for high-end restoration within a three-state radius, and nobody's meeting it properly. Because you're the best mechanic I've ever seen, and you're wasted on oil changes and brake jobs." He paused, his voice dropping. "And because I want you to have a reason to stay."

The last words hung between them, carrying more weight than any business proposition should.

"I'd need to think about it," Dylan managed.

"Of course. Take all the time you need. But Dylan—this isn't charity. This is a legitimate business opportunity that makes sense regardless of… anything else."

She knew what the "anything else" was—this thing building between them, slow and steady as restoration work itself.

"The Charger," she said, needing to shift to safer ground. "Would I get to restore it?"

"If you want to." His smile was quick and

genuine. "Consider it a signing bonus if you say yes."

As they walked back toward the house, Dylan's mind spun through possibilities. This wasn't just a job offer—it was everything she'd dreamed of, handed to her on terms that actually made business sense. She'd have the backing of The Pinnacle's reputation, steady income from regular work, and the freedom to build something of her own.

"Stay for coffee," Aidan said as they reached the kitchen door. "Mom made pie."

"I should go," Dylan said, overwhelmed by everything—the offer, the family, the way Aidan looked at her like she was already part of all this.

"Tomorrow then," he said. "Marcus needs your answer, doesn't he?"

She nodded, not trusting her voice.

"Whatever you decide, we're still hunting for that ring Saturday."

"Wouldn't miss it," she managed.

As she drove away from the O'Hara ranch, Dylan thought about the difference between running and choosing. Tomorrow she'd tell Marcus no. Not because she had to stay, but because she wanted to. Because Aidan had offered her not just a job but a future, not just work but the chance to build something lasting.

And maybe, just maybe, because the way he'd said "I want you to stay" sounded like the beginning of something worth staying for.

Monday arrived gray and promising rain, the mountains invisible behind clouds that pressed down like a weight. Dylan arrived at the garage at six, her usual time, but nothing felt usual anymore.

She'd made her decision sometime between leaving the O'Hara ranch and falling asleep in her newly painted bedroom. The restoration division wasn't just a good opportunity—it was the answer to a prayer she hadn't even known she'd been praying.

Marcus called at nine exactly.

"Dylan. Decision day."

She stood in her bay, looking at the Ferrari she'd perfectly repaired, at Ralph teaching Danny some arcane trick with a torque wrench, at Aidan through the office window, bent over paperwork with that concentration that made him look younger, more vulnerable.

"Thank you for the offer," she said, the words coming clear and certain. "But I'm going to stay in Laurel Valley. I've had a better offer here."

There was a pause. Then a chuckle. "O'Hara made you a better offer? Smart man. He knows talent when he sees it."

"You know Aidan?"

"I know of him. The Pinnacle's reputation reaches beyond state lines. If he's offering you a restoration division, you'd be a fool to turn it down."

"How did you—?"

"It's the logical next step for a shop like his. And with you running it? You'll have more work than you can handle within a year."

After she hung up, Dylan stood for a moment, feeling the weight of the decision settle into her bones. But it wasn't a heavy weight—it was an anchor, something to build on, something to keep her steady while she built something that mattered.

She knocked on Aidan's office door.

"Come in."

He looked up from his paperwork, and she saw the question in his eyes.

"The answer's yes," she said simply. "To the restoration division. To the partnership. To staying."

The smile that spread across his face was like sunrise after a long night—bright, warm, and full of promise.

"We should talk terms," he said, but he was already standing, already moving toward her.

"We should," she agreed, but she was smiling too, and for the first time in thirteen years, Dylan Flanagan felt like she was exactly where she was supposed to be.

Not running toward something or away from it, but standing still long enough to build something worth keeping.

Chapter Six

Tuesday evening painted Laurel Valley in shades of amber and rust, the October sun slanting through the mountains like it had all the time in the world. Dylan stood before her bedroom mirror, second-guessing her third outfit change and wondering when she'd become the kind of person who cared what she wore to a business dinner.

The burgundy sweater won—soft cashmere that Sophie had talked her into buying last year, insisting everyone needed at least one piece of clothing that made them feel powerful. Dylan had thought power came from competence, from skill, from being indispensable. She was learning it might also come from the way fabric moved against skin, the way color brought out hidden warmth, the way choosing to look beautiful was its own kind of bravery.

Her phone buzzed. Aidan—*Outside in five. We're walking—Main Street's too perfect tonight to waste.*

Through her window, she could see him already waiting on the sidewalk below, hands in the pockets of his leather jacket, head tilted back to study the sky like he was reading tomorrow's weather in tonight's clouds. Something about the way he stood—patient, comfortable, unhurried—made her chest tight with a feeling she refused to name.

The stairs creaked under her feet, each sound familiar as her own heartbeat. Five years of these stairs, but tonight they felt different. Tonight she was descending toward something more than dinner, more than business, more than the safe boundaries she'd maintained since arriving in Laurel Valley with nothing but grief and a determination never to need anyone again.

"Hey," Aidan said when she emerged, his smile warm as October sunlight. "You look—" He paused, seeming to catch himself. "Ready to make questionable business decisions?"

"The most questionable," she agreed, falling into step beside him.

Main Street stretched before them like a Halloween catalog come to life. Every storefront had embraced October with the fervor of true believers—corn stalks standing guard like scarecrow sentinels, pumpkins arranged in families of orange and white, wreaths woven from branches and berries that whispered autumn's secrets to anyone who passed close enough to hear.

The Lampstand glowed at the street's heart, its windows fogged with warmth and the steam of comfort food that had been drawing people for three decades. Through the glass, Dylan could see the Tuesday night regulars at their usual tables— the Martins celebrating their weekly date night, Bernie Watson holding court with his farming cronies, the book club ladies dissecting their latest romance novel with the intensity of scholars parsing ancient texts.

"Nervous?" Aidan asked as they approached the door.

"About signing contracts? No. About the entire town watching us have dinner and drawing conclusions? Terrified."

His laugh was rich as aged whiskey. "Welcome to Laurel Valley, where privacy is a four-letter word and everyone's business is community property."

Inside, The Lampstand enveloped them in its magic—the scent of herbs and possibility, the sound of laughter mixing with the clink of silverware, the warmth that came from more than just the kitchen's heat. Simone O'Hara materialized from the controlled chaos with the efficiency of someone who'd been reading a room since before Dylan was born.

"Aidan, Dylan." Her smile held layers, like she knew secrets they hadn't discovered yet. "Table for two?"

"For business," Aidan clarified, though the words sounded hollow even to Dylan's ears.

"Of course. Business." Simone led them through the restaurant with the confidence of a queen navigating her court, finally stopping at a corner booth partially hidden by an ornate wooden screen. "This should give you privacy for your…business discussion."

The booth was intimate in a way that had nothing to do with size and everything to do with atmosphere. Candlelight painted shadows on the dark wood, the noise of the restaurant faded to a comfortable murmur, and sitting across from Aidan felt suddenly, dangerously, like a date.

"So," Dylan said, needing to establish some kind of professional ground, "the contracts?"

Aidan pulled papers from his jacket with the solemnity of someone handling sacred texts. "Straightforward terms. I provide the initial investment for equipment, setup, everything needed to get operational. You run the restoration division with complete autonomy. Profits go first to recouping my investment, then we split fifty-fifty."

She read through the agreement, impressed by its clarity. No legal labyrinth, no hidden clauses, just two people agreeing to build something together.

"Why fifty-fifty?" she asked. "You're putting up all the money."

"You're putting up all the expertise. Money I can get anywhere. What you have—the skill, the eye, the ability to see what a rusted heap of metal could become—that's irreplaceable."

The compliment landed soft as snow, unexpected and warming. Dylan signed her name with steady hands, though her heart was attempting some kind of escape rhythm in her chest.

"Now we celebrate," Aidan said, signaling their waiter—a young man named James who looked like he'd rather be anywhere but serving food to people his parents' age. "Champagne?"

"It's Tuesday."

"It's the beginning of something extraordinary. Regular rules don't apply."

James brought champagne that sparkled like captured starlight, and Aidan raised his glass. "To partnership."

"To building something that matters," Dylan countered.

They drank, bubbles rising like hopes, like dreams, like all the possibilities they were too careful to name.

Their food arrived—short ribs for Aidan that fell apart at the touch of a fork, trout for Dylan that had been swimming that morning and now lay dressed in butter and herbs like a bridesmaid at autumn's wedding. They ate and talked business—equipment needs, potential clients, the timeline for getting operational—but underneath the practical discussion ran a current of something else, something that made every accidental touch of hands reaching for salt feel like lightning, every meeting of eyes across the table feel like confession.

"Can I ask you something?" Dylan said, setting down her fork. "You built The Pinnacle from nothing. Made it successful. Why add this complication now?"

Aidan turned his wine glass slowly, watching the light refract through the burgundy depths. "You ever feel like you're sleepwalking through your own life? Like you're successful at something you never actually chose?"

"Every day for thirteen years."

"Ten years ago, I came back from Denver with a business degree and a plan. The garage was practical, profitable, needed. I was good at it—the business side, anyway. Good with customers, good with numbers, good at the performance of being Aidan O'Hara, local boy made good." He paused, his eyes finding hers across the candlelight. "But watching you work, seeing how you approach restoration like it's sacred—it reminded me there's a difference between being successful and being alive."

"What changed?"

"That racing team offer I turned down eight years ago—I told everyone it was because of Dad's heart attack, and that was true. But it was also because I was scared. Scared of failing at something that mattered instead of succeeding at something safe."

"And now?"

"Now I want to try. To build something that's more than profitable. Something beautiful." The way he said *beautiful* while looking at her made Dylan's breath catch. "What about you? What made you finally say yes to staying?"

Dylan traced the rim of her glass, gathering words like scattered pearls. "I've been running since my father died. Not from anything specific, just from the possibility of loss. If you don't stay, nothing can leave you. If you don't care, nothing can hurt."

"Sounds lonely."

"It was. Is. But standing in your grandfather's ruins, seeing what your family built over centuries —I realized I've been so afraid of endings that I never allowed beginnings."

"And now?"

"Now I want to try. To see if I can build something that lasts longer than my fear."

They sat in comfortable silence, the weight of shared truth settling between them like sediment in still water. Around them, The Lampstand hummed with Tuesday night life—conversations rising and falling like waves, laughter punctuating the air like birdsong, the ordinary magic of people sharing food and time and stories.

"Walk with me," Aidan said after he'd paid the check, waving off her protests. "I want to show you something."

Outside, Main Street had transformed into something from a Halloween fairy tale. The decorations that seemed cheerful in daylight had become mysterious in darkness, shadows dancing between streetlights, jack-o'-lanterns grinning with ancient knowledge. The mountains pressed close, their darkness complete except for the occasional light from houses scattered like fallen stars on their slopes.

They walked in comfortable silence until Aidan stopped at an empty storefront three doors down from the garage. The windows were dark, dusty, forgotten looking, but he produced a key with the flourish of a magician revealing the prestige.

"What is this?" Dylan asked.

"Potential," he said, unlocking the door and finding the light switch.

The space exploded into visibility—high ceilings that seemed to reach toward heaven, original hardwood floors that had supported a century of dreams and failures, exposed brick walls that wore their age like dignity. It was raw, empty, waiting.

"When the restoration division outgrows its corner of The Pinnacle," Aidan said, "this could be yours. Your own space, your own shop."

Dylan walked through slowly, her footsteps echoing in the emptiness that felt full of tomorrow. She could see it already—the lift here, the office there, the reception area where she'd hang before-and-after photos like testimonies to transformation.

"You already bought it?"

"Option to buy. The owner's been trying to sell for two years. I wanted to secure the possibility."

"Why?" The word came out soft as prayer.

"Because I believe in you. In what you can build. Because—" He stopped, exhaling slowly. "Because I want you to have reasons to stay that have nothing to do with me but everything to do with who you could become here."

The honesty of it, the thoughtfulness, the way he was offering her dreams without strings—it all combined to crack something open in Dylan's chest, something she'd kept frozen since the night she'd watched her father's chest stop rising and falling and learned that love was just another word for loss.

"Thank you," she managed, the words inadequate for the gift he was offering.

"Thank you for staying long enough to accept it."

They stood in the empty space, future sprawling before them like an unmapped road. Dylan could feel the weight of possibility, the terrible beautiful burden of hope. This wasn't just about restoration anymore. This was about resurrection—of dreams, of faith, of the ability to believe that some things were worth the risk of wanting them.

"Your grandmother's diaries," she said, needing safer ground. "We should look through them for clues about where your grandparents met, where their love story began."

"Thursday night? After work? I'll make dinner —nothing fancy, but I can manage pasta without burning the house down."

"Your house?" The idea of being in his space, his private world, sent a thrill of danger through her.

"More room to spread out the documents. Plus, Mom left three boxes of family photos and papers when she heard about the treasure hunt. She's been waiting forty years for someone to care about family history."

They walked back toward her apartment, the October night wrapping around them like a shawl knitted from moonlight and woodsmoke. At her door, they paused, neither quite ready to end whatever this evening had become.

"Partners," Aidan said, and the word carried more weight than any contract could hold.

"Partners," Dylan agreed.

She climbed the stairs to her apartment, each step feeling like ascending toward something larger than herself. Inside, she stood at her window, watching Aidan walk back down Main Street, his figure gradually absorbed by darkness until only the memory of him remained.

Her phone lit up immediately:

Sophie—*The whole town is buzzing. Simone gave you the corner booth!*

Raven—*Just passed Aidan walking home. That man looked like he'd been hit by lightning in the best possible way.*

And from Aidan—*Thursday. 6 p.m. Bring your appetite for pasta and mysterious family history. This feels like the beginning of something important.*

Dylan set down her phone and looked around her apartment—walls now warm as embraces, space transformed from temporary to intentional. She'd signed contracts, made commitments, chosen to stay. But more than that, she'd chosen to hope.

Wednesday dawned crisp and clear, the kind of October morning that made the whole valley look like it had been painted by someone who understood that beauty and melancholy were sisters. Dylan arrived at the garage early, needing the familiar rhythm of work to steady herself against the changes she'd set in motion.

Ralph was already there, whistling something that might have been a love song or might have been a funeral dirge—with Ralph's musical ability, it was impossible to tell.

"So," he said, his mustache twitching with suppressed glee, "the corner booth."

"It was the only table available."

"That booth hasn't been 'available' since Simone took over. That's the booth where three generations of Laurel Valley couples have gotten engaged. There's actually a plaque."

"A plaque?"

"Tiny one. Brass. Says Love Starts Here in fancy script. Jimmy Chen had it made after he proposed to his wife there in '98."

Dylan focused intently on organizing tools that didn't need organizing. "It was a business dinner."

"Sure it was. And I'm a ballet dancer."

Before she could respond, Aidan appeared in the garage, morning light following him like a spotlight. He looked at her across the space, and his smile carried the memory of candlelight and confessions.

"Morning, partner," he said, and the word felt like a key turning in a lock, opening doors she'd kept closed for thirteen years.

"Morning," she managed, aware of Ralph watching them with the intensity of someone witnessing history.

"I've ordered the initial equipment for the restoration bay. Should be here Monday."

Monday. Five days away. Five days until the restoration division became real, concrete, undeniable. Five days to figure out how to be someone's partner without losing herself in the process.

"That's fast," she said.

"No point in waiting. We've got Mrs. Morrison's neighbor asking about a '67 Mustang, and Judge Hornsby wants to discuss his father's Packard. Word's already spreading."

Word was always spreading in Laurel Valley. By noon, three people had stopped by to congratulate Dylan on the partnership, two had asked if she was taking on apprentices, and Mrs. Whitfield from the historical society had called to say she had photographs of the O'Hara homestead from the 1920s that might help with the treasure hunt.

Dylan worked through it all, finding refuge in the familiar rhythm of diagnostics and repair. But her mind kept circling to Thursday, to dinner at Aidan's house, to the dangerous territory of his private space and family history.

The Ferrari owner finally arrived to collect his car, twelve days late and completely unapologetic. He handed over the payment without looking at the bill, his attention already on his next destination, his next forgettable adventure. Dylan watched him drive away and thought about the difference between moving and running, between traveling and searching, between being somewhere and belonging there.

"You okay?" Aidan asked, appearing at her shoulder with the stealth that seemed impossible for someone his size.

"Just thinking."

"Dangerous habit."

"Says the man who bought a building on potential."

"Secured an option on a building," he corrected. "There's a difference."

"Is there?"

He was quiet for a moment, and she could feel him choosing his words like selecting tools for a delicate repair. "One's a commitment. The other's a possibility. I wanted to give you possibilities, not obligations."

The thoughtfulness of it, the way he was trying not to pressure her even as he offered her dreams, made something shift in Dylan's chest like ice beginning its slow surrender to spring.

"Thursday," she said. "What should I bring?"

"Just yourself. And maybe wine if you don't trust my selection. Fair warning—I learned about wine from my brothers, which means I know exactly three facts and they're all wrong."

She laughed, and the sound surprised them both—free and genuine and carrying nothing but joy. It had been so long since she'd laughed like that, she'd forgotten the feeling of it, the way it loosened everything that had been held tight.

"I'll bring wine," she promised.

The rest of Wednesday passed in a blur of ordinary tasks made extraordinary by anticipation. Dylan found herself checking the clock, calculating hours until Thursday, until dinner, until the dangerous pleasure of being alone with Aidan in his space.

That night, she stood in her painted apartment, trying to see it through stranger's eyes. The terracotta walls glowed in lamplight, making the space feel like the inside of a heart. She'd hung a few pictures—nothing significant, just landscapes from the local art fair—but they transformed the walls from surfaces to stories.

This was what staying looked like. Small changes accumulating like snow, each one insignificant alone but together creating something that could alter landscapes. A painted wall here, a picture there, a business partnership, a dinner invitation—the architecture of a life being built choice by choice.

Her phone buzzed. Aidan: *Fair warning—I asked Mom for cooking advice and now the entire family knows you're coming for dinner Thursday. I expect at least three "casual" drop-bys.*

Dylan typed back—*Should I be worried?*

Only if you're allergic to aggressive matchmaking disguised as maternal concern.

I've survived this long in Laurel Valley. I think I've built up immunity.

We'll see. O'Hara women are varsity level. They've married off four sons. I'm the last holdout.

The last holdout. The words carried weight, significance, the shadow of the treasure hunt and

Patrick's hidden ring. Dylan wondered if Aidan knew how much his grandfather's game revealed —not just about the past but about the future Patrick had been trying to architect from beyond the grave.

Thursday came dressed in clouds that promised rain but couldn't quite deliver, the sky holding its breath like the whole valley was waiting for something to happen. Dylan worked through the day with half her attention, the other half already at dinner, already navigating the minefield of family history and personal boundaries.

At five thirty, she closed her toolbox with the finality of someone making a decision.

"Leaving early?" Ralph asked with studied innocence.

"I have dinner plans."

"I know. Everyone knows. Bernie Watson's taking bets on whether Anne shows up with dessert."

"What are the odds?"

"Three to one in favor. Better odds on Sophie arriving with wine recommendations."

Dylan shook her head, but she was smiling. This was the price of belonging—everyone in your business, everyone invested in your story, everyone hoping for your happiness with the fervor of people who understood that one person's joy lifted the whole community.

She went home to change, choosing jeans and a soft green sweater that made her eyes look even more violet. Nothing too fancy, nothing that suggested this was more than two friends researching family history. The lie was comfortable, necessary, as fragile as spun sugar.

The walk to Aidan's house took her away from downtown, into the residential streets where Laurel Valley's permanent residents made their lives. The houses here told stories—Craftsmans that had sheltered generations, Victorians that had been restored with love and money, new builds that tried to honor the town's architectural heritage with varying degrees of success.

Aidan's house sat on a corner lot, a 1920s bungalow that managed to be both modest and perfect. The porch light was on, warm and welcoming, and through the windows she could see him moving in what must be the kitchen, gesturing with a wooden spoon like he was conducting an orchestra or casting a spell.

She climbed the porch steps, wine bottle clutched like a talisman, and knocked.

"It's open," he called. "I'm at a critical pasta juncture and can't abandon my post."

Dylan let herself in, stepping into a space that was immediately, overwhelmingly Aidan. Books stacked on surfaces, a guitar leaning in the corner, photographs covering one wall like a collage of memory. But the couch looked like it had come with the house, the coffee table held more mail than personality.

"Kitchen's through here," he called. "Follow the smell of potential disaster."

She found him standing over a pot of boiling water, looking at it with the suspicion of someone who'd been betrayed by pasta before.

"How can you rebuild an engine from memory but look terrified of spaghetti?" she asked.

"Engines follow rules. Pasta is chaos pretending to be food." But he was smiling, relaxed in a way she'd never seen him, wearing jeans and a henley that had seen better decades.

"Fair warning—this is just my crash pad. I've got a place on the ranch, by the lake. That's home. But when I'm working late or there's an early meeting, it's easier to stay in town than make the drive out and back."

"So this is..."

"A place to sleep and shower. Maybe eat if I remember." He gestured at the sparse space with the wooden spoon. "The furniture came with the house. Seemed pointless to do more when I'm barely here."

"Wine," she said, offering the bottle. "To help or hinder, depending on your preference."

"Both. Always both."

He opened the wine with the efficiency of someone who'd learned that some skills were essential regardless of your interest in acquiring them. They drank while he finished cooking—a simple marinara that filled the kitchen with the scent of garlic and basil and home.

"The diaries are in the dining room," he said, stirring sauce with more concentration than the task required. "Mom brought three boxes. Apparently, she's been waiting for someone to show interest since approximately 1987."

They ate at his kitchen table, the pasta surprisingly good, the wine making everything softer, easier, more possible. Dylan found herself relaxing into the evening, into the simple pleasure of sharing food with someone who made her laugh, who looked at her like she was interesting, who offered her dreams without demanding payment.

After dinner, they spread the family documents across the dining room table—diaries, photographs, letters, the detritus of lives lived fully. Margaret O'Hara's diary was a treasure trove of daily life, observations of a world that no longer existed.

"Listen to this," Dylan said, reading from an entry dated 1962. "'Patrick took me to the old oak tree again today. He says it's our place, where our story began, but I think our story began the moment he walked into my father's store, hat in hand, trying to buy feed on credit. I knew then he was different. Knew then he was mine.'"

"The oak tree by the lake," Aidan said. "Has to be."

"But there's more. 'He carved our initials in the bark, high enough that we had to climb to see them. Said he wanted them to grow with the tree, to become part of something permanent.'"

They looked at each other across the table, understanding dawning. The next clue wasn't just hidden near the tree—it was in it, part of it, grown into its very fiber over decades.

"Saturday?" Aidan asked.

"Saturday," Dylan confirmed.

The evening had deepened into night without either of them noticing, too caught up in stories and secrets, in the mystery of how love persisted across decades, how some things endured despite everything time could throw at them.

"I should go," Dylan said, though leaving felt like tearing something.

"I'll walk you home."

"It's just right down the street."

"It's dark out. My mother raised me right, even if it didn't always take."

They walked down the street, quiet except for the small sounds of a town settling into sleep. At her door, they paused, the moment stretching like taffy, sweet and dangerous.

"Thank you," Dylan said. "For dinner. For the partnership. For believing I can do this."

"Thank you for staying," Aidan replied, and the words carried more weight than their simplicity suggested.

She climbed the stairs to her apartment, feeling his eyes on her until the door closed between them. Inside, she stood in the dark, processing the evening, the easy domesticity of it, the way being in his space had felt like coming home to a place she'd never been.

Saturday they would search for carved initials grown into bark, for evidence of love that had lasted. But Dylan was beginning to suspect they were really searching for permission—to hope, to trust, to believe that some things were worth the risk of wanting them.

The restoration division would launch Monday. The treasure hunt would continue Saturday. And somewhere between business and mystery, between partnership and possibility, Dylan Flanagan was falling further in love with Aidan O'Hara.

The terrifying part wasn't the falling.

It was how much she wanted to land.

FRIDAY ARRIVED WEARING FOG THICK AS WOOL, the mountains invisible behind curtains of white that turned Laurel Valley into an island floating in clouds. Dylan stood outside the Henderson building—what would become her restoration shop—watching Hank O'Hara measure doorways and tap walls with the focused intensity of a doctor examining a patient.

"The good news," Hank said, making notes on his tablet, "is the bones are solid. Better than solid. They built things to last in 1923."

"And the bad news?" Aidan asked from where he leaned against the brick exterior, looking unfairly good for seven in the morning.

"Those gorgeous hardwood floors have to go in the work areas. You can't put a two-post lift through hundred-year-old wood and expect it to hold. We'll need to excavate, pour reinforced concrete, proper drainage for the work bays."

Dylan tried not to let disappointment show. She'd been doing restoration work in a cramped corner of The Pinnacle for five years, making do with the standard garage equipment. When Aidan had shown her this space on Tuesday, she'd immediately envisioned keeping those floors, maintaining the building's character while creating something entirely hers.

"But," Hank continued, his expression softening at her obvious dismay, "we can save them in the front third of the building. Create zones—modern industrial in the back where you need it, historical preservation in front for your office, customer waiting area, display space. Best of both worlds."

"Display space?" Dylan asked.

"For before-and-after photos. Maybe a few choice pieces. You're not just fixing cars, you're creating art. People should see that the moment they walk in."

Aidan moved to stand beside her, close enough that she could feel his warmth in the cool morning. "What do you think?"

"I think it sounds expensive."

"Most things worth doing are." He turned to Hank. "Timeline?"

"If we start Monday, basic structural work will take three weeks. Electrical and plumbing, another two. You could be operational by Thanksgiving if we push, but I'd recommend waiting until after the holidays. Do it right rather than fast."

"After the holidays," Dylan agreed, though the wait chafed. She'd been ready for her own space for years; another two months felt like eternity.

"I'll draw up the plans this weekend," Hank said, tucking his tablet away. "Full restoration shop in back, elegant customer space in front. We'll expose those brick walls properly, keep the tin ceiling. It'll be the finest restoration shop in three states."

After Hank left for another job site, Dylan and Aidan stood alone in the foggy morning, looking at the building that would transform from abandoned storefront to dream realized.

"Second thoughts?" Aidan asked.

"Third and fourth thoughts. This is a massive investment."

"It's the right investment. You've been making do with a corner of The Pinnacle for five years. The work you've done—the Barracuda, the

Ferrari, all of it—that's been with basic equipment and borrowed space. Imagine what you'll create with a proper setup."

"What if—"

"Stop." He turned to face her fully, and the intensity in his green eyes made her words evaporate. "You're talented, Dylan. Beyond talented. You see what cars could be, not just what they are. This town needs that. I need that."

The last three words hung between them, weighted with meaning neither was ready to explore. Since Tuesday's dinner, since the signing of partnership papers and that walk through town, something had shifted. They were business partners now, but the air between them crackled with the possibility of something more.

"The equipment's already ordered," Aidan said, breaking the moment. "It'll go into storage until the renovation's complete. No point in setting it up at The Pinnacle just to move it. I may have gotten enthusiastic with the catalog."

"Aidan—"

"Partner's prerogative. Besides, Judge Harrison called yesterday about his Packard. He wants to be your first official restoration customer. That commission alone will cover the equipment costs."

Dylan felt overwhelmed by the speed of change, the weight of other people's faith in her abilities. "This is happening fast."

"Five years of groundwork isn't fast. It's overdue."

They walked back toward The Pinnacle together, navigating the foggy streets with the ease of people who knew every cobblestone, every uneven patch, every place where October ice liked to form. Downtown was beginning to wake—Rose arranging pastries in the bakery window, Bernie Watson setting up his newsstand, the town performing its morning ritual of transformation from sleeping beauty to bustling destination.

"Tomorrow," Aidan said as they reached the garage. "The treasure hunt continues."

Tomorrow. Saturday. The oak tree by the lake where Patrick had carved his initials with Margaret's, where love had been literally grown into the bark.

"Eight o'clock?" Dylan asked.

"I'll bring coffee and whatever my mother insists is necessary for treasure hunting."

"She knows?"

"She knows everything. It's actually a little creepy. She asked me yesterday if I'd found what I was looking for with this look that suggested she wasn't talking about the ring."

That evening, Sophie texted—*Wine at Raven's tonight. Just the O'Hara women. 7 p.m. No excuses.*

Dylan arrived at Raven's house—a stunning Victorian that Hank had restored with his typical attention to detail—to find the O'Hara women already gathered in the living room with enough wine bottles to stock a small vineyard.

"So," Raven said, elegant even in jeans and cashmere. "A restoration shop of your own. That's serious commitment to Laurel Valley."

"It's a business opportunity," Dylan said, aware of the undercurrents in the room.

"Of course it is," Sophie agreed with a smile that suggested she wasn't buying it. "Just like your dinner with Aidan on Tuesday was strictly business."

"We signed partnership papers."

"In the honeymoon booth at The Lampstand," Anne O'Hara added with maternal satisfaction. "Simone told me you two couldn't stop staring at each other."

Dylan felt heat climb her neck. "We were discussing terms."

"Is that what they're calling it now?" Raven laughed. "In my day, we just called it chemistry."

"Leave her alone," Sophie said, but her eyes danced with mischief. "She's only been here five years. Barely enough time to notice Aidan exists."

They laughed, and Dylan found herself smiling despite her embarrassment. This was what she'd missed in her years of running—the gentle teasing of women who cared, the assumption that her story was their story, that her happiness mattered to the collective whole.

Saturday dawned crystal clear, the fog burned away to reveal a world painted in October's finest palette. Frost silvered every surface, making the valley look like it had been dusted with diamonds. Dylan arrived at the lake turnout to find Aidan already there, leaning against his truck with two thermoses and a backpack that definitely contained more than necessary.

"Your mother?" she asked, gesturing at the pack.

"She heard we were hiking to the old oak. Apparently, that requires sandwiches, soup, first aid supplies, and emergency flares."

"Emergency flares. For walking fifty yards to a tree we can see from here."

"She worries. It's her superpower."

They walked toward the oak together, their breath clouding in the cold air, frost crunching under their boots. The tree stood magnificent against the morning sky, nearly bare now, its branches reaching toward heaven like prayers made solid.

"The initials should be…" Dylan circled the trunk, calculating growth patterns. "About twelve to fifteen feet up. Trees grow from the top, so what was eye level in 1962…"

"Is now completely unreachable." Aidan was already studying the branches, plotting his route. "Good thing I've maintained my climbing skills."

"When was the last time you climbed a tree?"

"Tuesday. Had to rescue Janice Plink's cat."

"That doesn't count."

"It does if the cat weighs twenty pounds and has opinions about being rescued."

He pulled himself up onto the lowest branch with surprising grace, muscles moving under his jacket in ways that made Dylan forget about treasure hunts entirely. She watched him climb, trying to focus on safety rather than the way he moved with such confident ease.

"Found them," he called from twelve feet up. "PMO + MES in a heart. God, Dylan, they're part of the tree now. The bark grew around them but preserved them perfectly."

"Is there anything else up there?"

"Looking." He checked the surrounding branches. "Nothing. But wait—Patrick was in his seventies when he hid these clues. He couldn't have climbed this high."

He climbed back down, and they both stood looking at the tree, thinking.

"The roots," Dylan said suddenly. "Check around the base, where the roots create natural hollows. That's where an older man could reach."

They searched the ground around the massive trunk, pushing aside years of accumulated leaves and forest debris. Dylan found it first—a depression between two large roots where the earth seemed disturbed.

"Here," she called.

Together they excavated the spot, finding a metal box wrapped in oilcloth and buried just deep enough to survive weather and time but shallow enough for an elderly man to manage.

Inside, wrapped in oilcloth, was another clue in Patrick's handwriting:

You found our hearts carved in the tree, / Now seek the place where we could see / The valley spread like promised land, / Where water mirrors sky so grand.

The chapel stone though walls have fell, / Where sacred vows were spoken well. / Find the altar where we knelt, / And know the love we truly felt.

Dylan read it twice, her mind working through the riddle. "A chapel with a view of the valley, near water."

"The old chapel ruins," Aidan said with sudden understanding. "By Mirror Lake, on the ridge. My great-great-grandfather built it in the 1880s for the family and ranch hands. Couples got married there for sixty years until it burned in 1945."

"How far?"

"About two miles up the northern trail. It's steep but beautiful. The foundation's still there, and the altar stone. On clear days you can see the entire valley reflected in the lake."

"Today?"

He looked at the sky, calculating. "It's a tough hike. Steep in places. We could wait until next Saturday."

It was the sensible choice. But standing there in the perfect morning with Aidan looking at her like she held answers to questions he hadn't asked yet, Dylan didn't want to be sensible.

"We have Anne's emergency supplies," she said. "Might as well use them."

His smile was slow and warm. "You sure?"

"I'm sure I want to know what happens next."

They set off up the trail, walking single file

where the path narrowed, then side by side as it widened. The forest closed around them, intimate as confession, the kind of quiet that made truth easier.

"Can I ask you something?" Aidan said after they'd been hiking for twenty minutes. "Why didn't you ever date anyone here?"

Dylan considered her answer. "I didn't plan to stay. Dating someone would have meant pretending I might."

"And now?"

"Now I'm opening a restoration shop and hunting for treasure with my business partner. Dating seems complicated."

They climbed in companionable silence, the trail growing steeper, more challenging. Dylan's legs burned, her breath came short, but she didn't complain. There was something cleansing about the effort, the simple goal of moving forward together.

The chapel ruins, when they finally reached them, were heartbreaking in their beauty. Stone walls stood open to the sky, Gothic arches framing views of the valley below and Mirror Lake spreading like liquid silver at the ridge's base. The altar stone remained intact, worn smooth by weather but still bearing the carved cross that had blessed generations of unions.

"This is where they started," Aidan said quietly. "Twenty years old, newly married, probably terrified."

Dylan walked through the ruins, her footsteps echoing on stone. Behind the altar, partially hidden by climbing ivy that had spent decades claiming the walls, she found a brass plaque green with age: *Patrick and Margaret O'Hara, married here June 21, 1962.*

"This is where they really began," she said softly.

Together they cleared away the leaves and forest detritus, revealing that the stone had been hollowed out beneath. Inside was another box, another piece of Patrick's elaborate puzzle.

But when Aidan opened it, there was no clue. Instead, there was a black-and-white photograph —Patrick and Margaret on their wedding day, radiant with certainty.

"Turn it over," Dylan said.

On the back, in Patrick's script: *The treasure isn't the ring. It's the reaching for it together. Next: Look for us where we said goodbye.*

Aidan's face changed. "The cemetery. She's buried at Mountain View. That's where the next clue must be."

The weight of it settled over them. Patrick had crafted a journey from life to death and back to life again, each clue revealing not just location but truth.

"Next Saturday?" Dylan asked gently.

"Next Saturday."

They stood in the ruins, afternoon light slanting through trees. The moment stretched between them, heavy with everything unsaid.

"Dylan," Aidan said, her name a question and answer both.

She turned to face him, finding him closer than expected, close enough to see gold flecks in green eyes, close enough to feel warmth in the cool air.

"This stopped being about business," he said quietly. "Tuesday, in the empty building, watching you see your future—I realized I want to be part of it. Not just as your partner. As more."

"Aidan—"

"I know it's complicated. I know we work together. I know there are a thousand reasons this is a bad idea." His hand came up to her face, fingertips barely grazing her cheek. "But standing here, where my grandparents started their life together with nothing but hope and stubbornness, I can't pretend I don't feel this."

Dylan's heart was attempting escape through her throat. Five years of watchful distance, and here they stood in ruins that had witnessed the beginning of a love that lasted sixty years.

"I don't know how to do this," she whispered.

"Neither do I. But maybe we can figure it out together."

The kiss was inevitable as sunrise—soft at first, cautious, then deeper as years of suppressed want demanded recognition. His hands framed her face like she was breakable and precious. Her hands found his chest, feeling his racing heart match hers.

When they pulled apart, breathless, the forest held its silence like approval.

"So," Dylan managed. "That happened."

"That definitely happened." His smile was crooked, uncertain, perfect. "Regrets?"

"Ask me when we're not standing in ruins in the middle of nowhere with your mother's emergency flares in our backpack."

They laughed, and it broke the tension without destroying the connection. They hiked back down together, hands occasionally brushing, occasionally holding, learning this new rhythm between them.

By the time they reached their vehicles, the sun was painting the sky in watercolors, and Dylan felt fundamentally changed, like something frozen had finally begun to thaw.

"Monday's going to be interesting," Aidan said.

"We're adults. We're professionals. We can handle it."

"Right. While the entire town watches and speculates and my mother starts planning our wedding."

"She wouldn't—" Dylan stopped at his expression. "She would."

"She's probably already chosen flowers."

They stood by their vehicles, neither ready to leave this bubble where kissing in ruins made perfect sense.

"Next Saturday," Aidan said. "The cemetery. We'll find the next clue."

"And then?"

"Then we figure out what comes next. The restoration shop, the partnership, us. All of it."

Dylan drove home through streets painted gold by dying light, her lips still tingling from the kiss, her mind spinning with implications. In two months, she'd have her own restoration shop. In a week, they'd search a cemetery for clues about a ring that had crossed oceans and centuries.

Chapter Eight

November arrived in Laurel Valley wearing frost like diamonds and carrying the scent of woodsmoke and promises of winter. Three weeks had passed since Dylan and Aidan's kiss among the chapel ruins—three weeks of exploration, of morning coffee that lingered longer than necessary, of dinners that danced on the edge of dates without quite committing to the label. They moved around each other with the delicate precision of people learning new rhythms, aware that the entire town watched with the fascination usually reserved for seasonal television dramas.

The restoration shop had consumed Dylan's daylight hours, offering refuge in physical progress from emotional uncertainty. Hank's crew had transformed the old Henderson building with the brutal efficiency of men who understood that sometimes destruction preceded resurrection. They'd torn up the beautiful hardwood floors in the work areas, jackhammered through decades of patches and amateur repairs, and poured new concrete that could support the weight of lifted vehicles and lifted dreams in equal measure.

The front third of the building had been preserved like a love letter to the past—those gorgeous hardwood floors refinished until they glowed like honey in sunlight, the tin ceiling restored to its pressed-metal glory, the brick walls exposed and sealed to show every nuance of age and endurance. It was becoming exactly what Dylan had envisioned: a place where past and present shook hands, where restoration was revealed as the art it had always been.

She stood now in what would be her office, watching snow begin its slow descent through the large front window. The first real snow of the season, arriving with November's authority, transforming Laurel Valley into something from a child's dream of winter—perfect, pristine, impossibly pure. Behind her, the work bays echoed with the percussion of progress as contractors installed the lift system, each clang and drill whir a note in the symphony of becoming.

"It's magnificent," Aidan said from the doorway, and she didn't need to turn to know he was smiling. She'd learned to read his voices like sheet music—this one carried pride seasoned with something warmer, something that had been simmering since their kiss but remained unspoken, like bread rising in secret.

"Four more weeks, according to Hank." Dylan traced a finger along the window, following a snowflake's fatal descent. "Then I can officially open Dylan's Restoration—though I'm still not sold on the name."

"What about Flanagan's Restorations? Classic, timeless."

"Too formal. Like I should be wearing a monocle and discussing the Habsburg dynasty."

His laugh filled the space between them, warm as August in November's chill. "The Restoration Mill? Playing off the valley's history?"

"Better. But still not quite right." She turned to face him, finding him closer than expected, close enough that she could see snowflakes caught in his hair like nature's confetti. "We missed Saturday again."

Three Saturdays had passed without returning to their treasure hunt. First, the restoration shop's plumbing crisis that had flooded the back bay.

Then Aidan's trip to the classic car auction in Bozeman where he'd bought three vehicles for future restoration. Last week, an early storm that had made the mountain trails treacherous with ice and bad decisions. Excuses dressed as reasons, all of them, but easier than facing what finding that ring might mean, what claiming it might promise.

"Next weekend?" Dylan suggested, the same words she'd offered for three weeks running.

"Next weekend," he agreed with equal practice. "Though at this rate, we'll be treasure hunting in snowshoes."

They stood in comfortable silence, watching November paint the world white through the window. Dylan had learned to treasure these quiet moments—the spaces between words where understanding grew like mushrooms in darkness, where friendship deepened into something neither quite dared name aloud.

"Dinner tonight?" Aidan asked. "Simone's making that butternut squash soup you love."

"I'm working late," she said, disappointed. "The McLaren's owner wants it Monday, and there's an engine harmonic that's driving me insane."

"I could bring you something. Save you from starvation."

"You don't have to—"

"I want to." He turned to face her fully, and something in his expression made her breath catch like a skipped heartbeat. "Dylan, I—"

"Mr. O'Hara?" One of Hank's workers materialized in the doorway like an interruption incarnate. "Your brother needs you to check the placement of the alignment rack."

The moment shattered like an icicle hitting pavement. Aidan stepped back, the almost-words hanging between them like snow suspended in air, waiting to fall.

"I'll see you later," he said, and Dylan nodded, not trusting her voice to remain steady.

She returned to The Pinnacle as afternoon deepened toward evening, losing herself in the familiar rhythm of diagnostics. The Ferrari's engine was a puzzle wrapped in Italian engineering and expensive anxiety—its strange harmonic occurring only at specific RPMs, only when the engine was warm, only when Mercury was in retrograde and the garage spirits were feeling capricious.

The garage had gone quiet, Ralph and Danny long departed to their families and lives that existed beyond timing belts and torque specifications. Dylan worked in the pool of light from her work lamp, the world narrowed to the engine bay and the elusive sound that shouldn't exist but stubbornly did.

She was so absorbed in the hunt that she didn't hear the footsteps until they stopped directly behind her—expensive heels on concrete, a sound that didn't belong in the garage's usual symphony.

"Excuse me?"

Dylan straightened and turned to find a woman who looked like she'd been assembled by a committee tasked with defining winter elegance. Tall, blond, wearing a coat that probably cost more than Dylan's monthly expenses, with the kind of bone structure that made other women immediately aware of their own facial inadequacies. This was a woman who'd never met a mirror that didn't love her back.

"We're closed," Dylan said, wiping her hands on a shop rag that seemed to be redistributing grease rather than removing it.

"I'm looking for Aidan O'Hara." The woman's voice carried the polish of expensive education and breeding, but underneath lurked something else—determination wearing nervousness like camouflage.

"He left about an hour ago. I can take a message."

The woman studied Dylan with eyes the color of winter sky, cataloguing the coveralls, the grease, the defensive posture of someone protecting their territory. "You must be the new mechanic. Diana?"

"Dylan."

"Right. Dylan." She extended a manicured hand that had never met a callus. "I'm Victoria Pemberton. Aidan and I are…old friends."

The name landed like snow on bare skin—shocking, cold, immediately seeping into uncomfortable recognition. Dylan had heard it whispered in the corners of town gossip, passed between coffee cups and over shop counters. Victoria Pemberton, the one who got away—or threw him away, depending on the narrator's romantic philosophy. The woman everyone had expected Aidan to marry before she'd chosen Manhattan over mountains.

"He's probably at home by now," Dylan managed, proud that her voice remained level as a balanced engine.

"I tried there first. His neighbor said he was probably here or at The Lampstand." Victoria smiled, and it was the kind of smile that had probably opened doors, hearts, and bank vaults with equal ease. "I was hoping to surprise him."

"Mission accomplished, I'm sure."

Victoria tilted her head, studying Dylan with renewed interest, like a cat discovering an unexpected mouse. "Have we met? There's something familiar about you."

"I don't travel in circles that require that much dry-cleaning."

"No, I suppose not." But the assessment in her eyes suggested she was recalculating something, adjusting her equations. "How long have you worked for Aidan?"

"Five years. And I work with him, not for him."

"Of course. My mistake." She pulled out her phone with the efficiency of someone who'd never been without immediate communication. "Well, I'll just text him myself. We have some business to discuss."

Before Dylan could respond, headlights swept across the garage entrance like searchlights seeking truth. Aidan's truck pulled in, and Dylan watched him emerge carrying a takeout bag from The Lampstand. He'd brought her dinner, just as promised. The simple thoughtfulness of it, the casual care, made something in her chest constrict.

He stopped when he saw Victoria, his whole body going still in a way Dylan had never witnessed—like a deer caught not in headlights but in the scope of something more dangerous.

"Tori?"

"Hello, Aidan." Victoria moved toward him with the confidence of someone who'd never been turned away from anything she wanted. "Surprise."

Dylan watched them embrace—brief, formal, with the awkwardness of people trying to navigate the ghost of former intimacy. She turned back to the Ferrari, giving them privacy while her hands worked on autopilot.

"What are you doing here?" Aidan's voice carried shock layered over something harder to identify—not pleasure, not quite displeasure, but the wariness of someone finding a door they'd locked standing open.

"Daddy's not well. Heart problems. I've taken a leave from the firm to help him manage things." Victoria's voice softened strategically. "It's been seven years, Aidan. I thought enough time had passed that we could be civil."

"We can be civil from a distance. We've been doing it successfully for seven years."

The coldness in his tone made Dylan glance over, surprised. This wasn't the easy-going Aidan she knew. This was someone who'd been hurt and had decided not to offer a second chance for the experience.

"People change," Victoria said, though something in her perfect composure cracked slightly.

"Do they? You left because Laurel Valley was too small, too limiting, too…" He paused. "How did you put it? Suffocatingly quaint?"

"I was twenty-eight. I thought ambition was everything."

"And now?"

"Now I'm thirty-five and realized ambition is lonely without someone to share the success."

Dylan's hands stilled on the engine. She shouldn't be listening to this, but the garage's acoustics made privacy impossible.

"Dylan," Aidan said, and she had to turn, had to face them. Victoria looked like winter personified—beautiful and cold. Aidan looked like a man who'd found his past waiting in his present and wasn't happy about the reunion. "This is Victoria Pemberton. Victoria, this is Dylan Flanagan, my business partner. She runs our restoration division."

Something flickered across Victoria's perfect features—surprise, calculation, reassessment. "Partner. How interesting." Her gaze swept over Dylan with new interest, the kind that made Dylan acutely aware of the grease under her fingernails. "The restoration market is exploding in certain circles. Daddy's investment group is very interested in sustainable luxury businesses."

"We're not looking for investors," Aidan said firmly, moving to stand closer to Dylan. "We have everything we need."

"Of course. But markets change, businesses grow. If you ever want to expand beyond…" she gestured vaguely at the garage, managing to make it sound like a small, backwoods shop despite its success, "…I'm here for at least a month while Daddy recovers."

She pulled out a business card with a flourish that belonged on a stage. "My cell's on there. It would be nice to catch up, Aidan. Seven years is a long time to leave things unsaid."

"Some things are better left buried," Aidan said quietly. "I hope your father recovers quickly."

Victoria's perfect smile faltered like a lightbulb flickering before failure. "Well. I see. Nice to meet you, Dylan."

She left in a cloud of expensive perfume and disappointed expectations, her heels clicking away like a countdown to complications.

Aidan stood frozen for a moment, then seemed to remember the takeout bag growing cold in his hand. "I brought soup. And those breadsticks you pretend you don't love."

"I don't pretend anything about breadsticks. Our love is pure and public."

He laughed, and the tension in the garage eased like a released breath. "I should explain about Victoria."

"You don't owe me explanations."

"Yes, I do." He set the bag on the workbench, then turned to face her fully. "We're partners. We're…" He paused, searching for words like a mechanic feeling for the right socket in the dark. "We're whatever we're becoming. You should know that Victoria and I dated seven years ago. For two years. Everyone thought we'd get married. Then she got a job offer in New York, said Laurel Valley could never give her the life she wanted. She left. We haven't spoken since."

"And now she's back."

"Temporarily. For her father." He moved closer, close enough that Dylan could see the strain around his eyes. "This doesn't change anything, Dylan. Not the partnership, not the restoration shop, not…"

"Not what?"

"Not the fact that I haven't been able to stop thinking about kissing you again since the chapel ruins."

The words hung between them like snow balanced on a branch—beautiful, precarious, ready to fall at the slightest disturbance.

"Aidan—"

"I know. I know we agreed to take things slow. I know we're business partners. I know there are a hundred reasons why this is complicated." His hand came up, not quite touching her face, hovering like a question. "But Victoria showing up reminded me that time passes. Opportunities disappear. People leave. And I don't want to waste any more time pretending I don't feel what I feel."

Dylan's heart was attempting to break free from her rib cage. "Which is?"

"Like you're the first person I want to tell when something good happens. Like the garage feels empty when you're not here. Like I've been waiting my whole life for someone who looks at a broken car and sees what it could become, who understands that restoration isn't about making something new but honoring what it's always been."

The Ferrari engine ticked as it cooled, marking time in metallic whispers. Outside, snow continued to fall, insulating them from the world beyond the garage doors.

"I'm scared," Dylan admitted, the words scraping past years of carefully constructed walls.

"Me too. But my grandfather always said the best things usually are scary. That's how you know they matter."

He was so close now she could feel the warmth radiating from him, could count the snowflakes melting in his hair. The moment stretched between them, taut as a timing belt about to snap.

"The soup's getting cold," Dylan said, but she didn't move away.

"It's supposed to be cold. It's gazpacho."

"It's butternut squash."

"Then it's definitely getting cold."

They stood there, inches apart, both smiling at the absurdity of discussing soup temperature when the air between them crackled with enough electricity to power the entire valley.

"Eat your dinner," Aidan said finally, stepping back with visible effort. "Fix the Ferrari. I'll lock up the front."

Dylan unwrapped the soup—still warm despite their debate—and ate while working, her mind spinning faster than any engine. Victoria was back. Beautiful, polished, historically significant Victoria who'd shared two years of Aidan's life before Dylan had even known Laurel Valley existed.

But Aidan had sent her away. Had stood in his own garage and chosen the present over the past, had moved closer to Dylan rather than toward his history. That had to mean something.

The McLaren's harmonic revealed itself finally, a loose heat shield vibrating at exactly the wrong frequency. Dylan fixed it with three well placed welds, solving in minutes what had puzzled her for hours. Sometimes the answer was simpler than expected. Sometimes it was right in front of you, waiting to be discovered.

She finished near midnight, the garage silent except for the tick of cooling metal and the whisper of snow against windows. Her phone buzzed as she cleaned her tools.

Aidan—*Home safe? The roads are getting slick.*

Then another—*Thank you for listening tonight. For not running when Victoria showed up.*

And finally—*Saturday. No more excuses. We find the next clue. We figure out what we're doing. Both things. All things.*

Dylan typed back—*Saturday. Bring rope.*

Rope?

In case we need to escape through windows when your ex-girlfriend shows up at the cemetery.

That's morbid. Also hilarious. Also possible knowing Victoria.

Saturday, Dylan typed again, then added, *Partner.*

The word carried new weight now, loaded with possibility and promise and the particularly terrifying hope that some things might be worth the risk of wanting them.

She locked the garage and walked home through the falling snow, her footsteps the only marks on Main Street's white canvas. The town had dressed itself for November while she'd been working—Thanksgiving wreaths glowing warm in windows, cornucopias spilling abundance onto doorsteps, the pumpkins of Halloween replaced by the deeper satisfaction of harvest home.

Her apartment welcomed her with terra-cotta warmth, the walls she'd painted now feeling less like commitment and more like embrace. Dylan stood at her window, looking down at Main Street's empty perfection, and let the doubts she'd been holding back flood in.

Victoria Pemberton. Even the name sounded like it belonged in a different world than Dylan Flanagan. Victoria probably had childhood photos on horses, debutante balls, the kind of education that taught you which wine went with which course. She definitely didn't have grease permanently embedded under her fingernails or a father who'd died leaving nothing but debt and a collection of motorcycle parts.

Dylan caught her reflection in the dark window—tired eyes, hair escaping from its ponytail, the shadows of old oil stains on her jaw that never quite washed clean. She looked exactly like what she was: a mechanic who'd gotten lucky. Meanwhile, Victoria looked like what Aidan should have on his arm at charity galas and family Christmas cards.

Seven years. They'd been apart seven years, but history like that didn't just evaporate. First loves lived in your bones, shaped the way you loved everyone who came after. And Victoria had been Aidan's first real love—the one everyone expected him to marry, the one who'd fit into his world like she'd been custom-made for it.

What if his rejection tonight had been about pride, not preference? What if seeing Victoria again reminded him of what he'd given up, what he could have had? Beautiful, sophisticated Victoria who knew about cars and probably spoke three languages and definitely never had to google which fork to use first.

Dylan moved to her bathroom mirror, studying herself critically. She could clean up well enough—Sophie had proven that with a few shopping trips—but underneath the surface polish, she was still the girl who'd run from her father's funeral, who'd spent thirteen years never staying anywhere long enough to matter. Victoria had roots, connections, the kind of deep belonging that Dylan was only just beginning to attempt.

Her phone sat silent on the counter. Aidan's texts glowed on the screen, sweet and reassuring. But texts were easy. Words were easy. Tomorrow, in daylight, when Victoria probably stopped by the garage in some perfect outfit with some perfect excuse, would Aidan still stand closer to Dylan? Or would he remember what he'd lost, what he could have again?

Dylan turned away from the mirror, unable to bear her own reflection any longer. She was building something here—a business, a life, maybe even a future with someone who made her heart race. But Victoria's arrival felt like a reminder that some people were meant for permanent things and others were just passing through, no matter how much paint they put on the walls.

Change was coming—it always did when old lovers returned and new possibilities emerged. But standing in her painted apartment, with partnership papers on her table and Aidan's texts on her phone, Dylan felt something she hadn't experienced in the thirteen years since her father's death:

Ready.

Ready for whatever Victoria's presence might stir up. Ready for the restoration shop to open. Ready to find the next clue and the one after that. Ready to stop running from the possibility that some things—some people, some places, some feelings—might be worth the risk of staying still long enough to see what grew.

Outside, November continued its patient work of transformation, covering everything complicated with simple white, hiding all the broken places under beauty. By morning, Laurel Valley would look like a postcard, the kind people sent to prove that perfect places existed.

But Dylan knew better. She knew perfection was overrated. What mattered was the willingness to restore what was broken, to see potential in damage, to believe that with enough care and skill and patience, anything could be made beautiful again.

Even hearts that had forgotten how to trust.

Even partnerships that might be becoming something more.

Even small mountain towns where past and present collided like weather fronts, creating storms that cleared the air for whatever came next.

Chapter Nine

SATURDAY MORNING SLIPPED INTO DYLAN'S apartment like silk through fingers—soft, inevitable, impossible to hold. She'd been awake since four, watching November darkness fade to the pearl gray that preceded dawn, her mind circling the same territory it had worn smooth over three sleepless nights. Victoria Pemberton had arrived in Laurel Valley like winter itself—beautiful, cold, and capable of changing everything with her presence.

The drive to the O'Hara ranch wound through a valley still drowsing under frost, each surface transformed to crystal, catching early light like the earth had been dressed in diamonds for some celebration Dylan hadn't been invited to. The ranch gates stood open as always, a testament to the O'Haras' bone-deep confidence that what was theirs would remain so—a certainty Dylan envied with an ache that sat just behind her ribs.

She found Aidan waiting at the family cemetery entrance, two thermoses steaming in the cold air, his expression carrying the weight of someone who'd been building toward difficult words.

"Thought you might not come," he said, offering her coffee that smelled like comfort and complicated futures.

"Said I would."

"You've said a lot of things this week. Also avoided saying a lot of things." His green eyes held hers with an intensity that made her want to inventory everything she'd ever done wrong. "Talk to me, Dylan. Is this about Victoria?"

The directness of it—so unlike their usual tap dance around feelings—caught her unprepared. "I've been busy with the restoration shop."

"Dylan." Just her name, but weighted with three days of her strategic absences, of taking lunch at odd hours, of finding urgent tasks whenever he appeared.

"Sophie saw her going into The Pinnacle yesterday afternoon."

His jaw tightened, a muscle jumping in a way she'd learned meant he was choosing words carefully. "She stopped by. Wanted to discuss investment opportunities. I told her we weren't interested and that I had actual work to do."

"And?"

"And nothing. She left. That's where it ended."

"Is it?"

He moved closer, bringing that intoxicating mixture of pine soap and possibility that had been undermining her defenses for five years. "Yes. Victoria is my past—a choice I made when I thought life was about what looked right rather than what felt right. You're my present. Hopefully my future, if you'll stop running long enough to let it happen."

The words settled over her like snow—soft, transformative, impossible to brush away without leaving evidence of their touch.

They entered the cemetery through gates that sang hymns to the wind, the O'Hara family plot occupying the highest ground like even in death they claimed the best views. Generations rested here in clusters that suggested affection transcending mortality, the oldest stones worn smooth as river rocks, their names more memory than fact.

Margaret O'Hara's granite marker stood beside Patrick's, elegant in its simplicity, the dates telling a love story in numbers—fifty-six years together before she passed.

"The clue should be here somewhere," Aidan said, examining the area with the focus he usually reserved for stubborn engine problems. "But Grandda was in his seventies. He couldn't have done anything too physical."

Dylan's eye caught on an ornate iron cross standing between the headstones—Victorian elaborate, the kind of memorial wealthy families commissioned when death was dressed in poetry rather than avoided in silence. But something about its base seemed wrong. Newer.

"There," she said, kneeling to examine it closer.

They found what Patrick intended—a bronze plaque that appeared decorative but opened on hidden hinges, revealing another clue wrapped in waterproof cloth.

Where love was witnessed by the stars, / And sacred vows were made, / Not in the chapel or the church, / But where the moonlight played. / The garden holds its secrets still, / Though roses bloom no more, / Find the sundial's shadow when / The clock strikes exactly four.

"Grandma's moon garden," Aidan said immediately, his voice carrying the resonance of memory made physical. "She planted it their first year of marriage—all white flowers that bloomed at night, designed to be beautiful in moonlight."

They left the cemetery with appropriate reverence, walking back toward where the ranch vehicles were kept. The morning had warmed enough to make Dylan's jacket unnecessary, and she felt Aidan watching as she tied it around her waist, his gaze carrying weight that had nothing to do with outdoor apparel.

"We could walk to the garden," he suggested. "But it's two miles of rough trail. Or we could take the ATVs."

"Let's ride."

The barn smelled of hay and machine oil, horse and history. Dylan immediately moved to the newer ATV, checking it over with professional interest that made Aidan smile.

"Most people just get on and ride," he observed.

"Most people aren't mechanics. "

They set off across property that seemed to expand with every hill they crested, following trails worn by generations of O'Hara adventures. The freedom of it—racing through private land with no witnesses except mountains and sky—loosened something that had been twisted tight in Dylan's chest since Victoria's appearance. When Aidan took a trail that launched them over a rise, she followed without hesitation, both machines leaving earth for a moment that felt like flight, landing hard enough to jar teeth but laughing at the sheer joy of controlled recklessness.

They stopped at a creek to rest, sitting on sun-warmed rocks that November hadn't yet stolen heat from, watching water write stories over stones.

"Haven't seen you smile like that in days," Aidan said, pulling off his helmet to reveal hair standing in every direction like he'd been electrocuted by happiness.

"Haven't had much reason to."

"Victoria really rattled you."

It wasn't a question, but Dylan answered anyway. "She's everything I'm not. Polished, sophisticated, from your world—"

"Stop." The command in his voice made her look at him fully. "Victoria is from a world I was supposed to want. You're from the world I actually want. There's a difference between choosing what looks right and choosing what is right."

Before she could parse that declaration,

another ATV's growl announced company. Duncan appeared through the trees, his grin promising trouble or gossip or both.

"Thought I heard engines," he said, pulling up beside them. "Hattie sent me to find you. She said I'm getting too moody because I'm having trouble with a commissioned piece. I don't get moody."

He scowled and Aidan laughed. "Whatever you say, brother. What's the news?"

"Hattie wanted to warn you. She said Victoria's been making rounds in town, asking subtle questions about Dylan at various shops. Everybody remembers Victoria and the way she left, so I'm not sure she's being met with a lot of warmth, but you know how people here like to talk."

"Like it's fresh air?" Aidan asked.

Dylan's stomach performed an unpleasant maneuver. "She's investigating me?"

"More like fishing for information. But Sophie and Raven are onto her. They're telling her how famous people from all over the country are clamoring for you to restore their cars."

"It was only one famous person," Dylan said.

"I'm sure there are more where that came from," Duncan said. "Raven told her about how the Smithsonian asked you to consult on a vintage restoration project."

"Oh, God," Dylan said, covering her face with her hands.

"You do good work," Duncan said. "Be proud. And you'll get used to Raven and Sophie. That's what family does. We protect our own."

After he left, they continued to the moon garden, but Dylan's mind kept circling back to Victoria's reconnaissance mission, the way she was gathering intelligence like this was some kind of campaign for territory that had already been claimed.

The garden, when they reached it, temporarily erased all thoughts of Victoria. It was magnificent in its architecture—geometric beds outlined in boxwood that had survived for decades, paths of stone and gravel, and in the center, a sundial on a pedestal that had been marking time since long before Dylan was born.

"She designed it herself," Aidan said, moving through the space with the respect of someone in a museum. "Every plant chosen for how it looked in moonlight. They'd sit out here summer nights, just watching stars and each other. My mother has kept it up since Grandma passed, though she'll tell you she doesn't have as green of a thumb."

"It's beautiful," Dylan said, already seeing the potential beneath the ruin.

They settled on a bench near the sundial to wait for four o'clock, time stretching before them like an unmapped road.

"Tell me something I don't know about you," Aidan said, his thigh warm against hers on the cold stone bench.

"Like what?"

"Anything. Everything. Why you became a mechanic. What you dream about. What you're afraid of."

Dylan pulled her knees up, wrapping her arms around them in a defensive posture she hadn't needed in years. "My father was a mechanic. After my mother left—I was ten—working on engines was the only time he seemed truly alive. Not happy, exactly, but…purposeful. I learned by watching, by handing him tools, by being useful in the only way that seemed to matter."

"She left you both?"

"Decided she wanted more than a mechanic husband and a daughter who preferred grease to dolls. We weren't enough for her vision of life."

Dylan remembered the morning her mother left with the clarity that only trauma provides—standing in the kitchen doorway with two suitcases, wearing the pearl earrings Dad had saved six months to buy. Her lipstick was perfect, a red Dylan would later see on other women and feel her stomach clench.

"Take care of your father," she'd said, not quite meeting Dylan's eyes. "You're more like him anyway."

The words had been meant as explanation but landed like prophecy. Dylan had become exactly that—her father's keeper through the good years, then his nurse through the bad ones. She'd learned to read his silences, to know which meant contentment and which meant the hollow ache of abandonment. They'd developed their own language in the garage, one built of socket wrenches and comfortable quiet, of teaching moments that were really about holding on to something solid while everything else felt untethered.

"When the cancer diagnosis came," Dylan said quietly, "he apologized to me. Can you imagine? Dying man apologizing to his twenty-two-year-old daughter for the inconvenience of his mortality." Her voice caught. "He was more worried about me being stuck taking care of him than about his own death. Said he didn't want me to waste my youth changing his bedpans and fighting with insurance companies."

She paused, remembering those last months with a vividness that still stole her breath. "But I wasn't stuck. I was terrified. Every morning I'd stand outside his door, listening for breathing, bargaining with a God I wasn't sure existed for just one more day. One more joke about my terrible coffee. One more argument about the proper way to gap spark plugs. One more anything."

The weight of those days settled over her—the smell of antiseptic mixing with motor oil, the way his hands had thinned until his wedding ring slipped off and he'd asked her to put it somewhere safe, not realizing he was asking her to acknowledge the ending.

"The last six months were the worst," she continued. "He couldn't work anymore, could barely hold tools. For a man who'd defined himself by what his hands could fix, it was its own kind of death before the actual one. I kept the shop running, lied to his customers, said he was just slow on their repairs, not dying by degrees in the apartment above. He made me promise to finish every project. Said a mechanic's reputation was all they left behind."

Her hands clenched involuntarily, remembering. "The night he died, he asked me to bring him a torque wrench. Just wanted to hold it. His fingers could barely close around it, but he smiled like I'd brought him salvation. 'At least I'll die with clean hands for once,' he said. I laughed—God help me, I actually laughed—because even with the morphine eating holes in his awareness, he could still make jokes. He died two hours later, still holding that wrench, and I sat there until dawn, afraid that if I took it from his hands, he'd really be gone."

She looked at Aidan then, her eyes bright with unshed tears. "I finished every project in that shop. Delivered the last car the day after his funeral. Then I packed everything I could fit in my Charger and ran. I've been running ever since, because staying means watching things end, and I'd already watched the two most important people in my life leave—one by choice, one by force. I couldn't do it again."

"Is that why you run? Because you watched him wait?"

The question cut deeper than intended, finding the soft place she'd protected for thirteen years. "I run because staying hurts more when it ends. And everything ends, Aidan. Your grandfather's treasure hunt is literally about finding a ring in a cemetery where the love story is already over."

"No," he said with surprising firmness. "It's about finding a ring that survived the ending. That continues, waiting for the next story. Love doesn't die just because people do."

They sat in comfortable silence while shadows crept across the sundial face like time made visible. Sophie appeared at some point with a picnic basket, took one look at their proximity on the bench, and left with a smile that promised immediate family-wide notification.

At four o'clock exactly, they watched the shadow align with a mark on the sundial's base. When Aidan pressed it, nothing happened.

"Try again," Dylan said, kneeling beside him.

He pressed harder. A soft click, but still nothing opened.

"Wait." Dylan ran her fingers along the sundial's base, feeling for irregularities. "There—feel that? There's another mark here, at two o'clock."

"So maybe we need to—" Aidan checked his watch. "We missed it. Two o'clock was hours ago."

"No, look at the design." Dylan traced the ornate metalwork around the sundial's face.

"These aren't just decorative. They're Roman numerals worked into the pattern. What if we need to press them in sequence?"

They studied the sundial together, heads nearly touching. The Roman numerals were cleverly hidden in the scrollwork—IV disguised as part of a vine, IX worked into a flower's petals.

"Four o'clock," Dylan said. "IV. Then what?"

"The clue mentioned sacred vows. Marriage vows." Aidan's eyes lit up. "My grandparents' anniversary—June 21st. Six and twenty-one. VI and…there's no twenty-one in Roman numerals on a sundial."

"But two and one," Dylan said suddenly. "II and I. Press them separately?"

Aidan found the hidden II worked into what looked like parallel stems. "Got it. So IV, then VI, then II, then I?"

They pressed the sequence. Another click, louder this time, and a section of the pedestal shifted but didn't open.

"We're close," Dylan said. "But something's still missing."

She stood back, studying the whole structure. The sundial sat on an octagonal base, each face decorated with different scenes—gardens, mountains, water, stars.

"The clue," she said. "Where love was witnessed by the stars. Which face has stars?"

They circled the pedestal. The north face showed a night sky worked in metal, constellation patterns picked out in tiny holes that would let light through.

"Press the same sequence on this side," Dylan suggested.

This time, when they completed the sequence, the entire north face of the pedestal swung open on hidden hinges, revealing not just one compartment but three, each with its own small lock.

"Of course it couldn't be simple," Aidan muttered. "Three locks, no keys."

Dylan examined the locks closely. "Not key locks. These are puzzle locks. Look—each has different symbols."

The first showed phases of the moon, the second had seasons represented by tiny leaves, snowflakes, flowers, and fruit. The third displayed numbers in what looked like dates.

"The moon garden," Dylan said. "Full moon for the first—that's when the white flowers bloomed best."

The second lock clicked open when Aidan turned it to summer—when they were married.

"The third has to be their wedding date," he said, spinning the numbers to 06-21-62.

All three compartments opened simultaneously, but only the middle one contained anything —another oilcloth bundle with the next clue.

"Your grandfather really didn't want this found by accident," Dylan said.

"He wanted it found by someone willing to work for it," Aidan corrected. "By people working together. I couldn't have solved this alone."

Dylan felt the weight of that statement—the way it applied to more than just puzzle locks and hidden compartments. She watched as Aidan carefully lifted the oilcloth bundle from the middle compartment, his hands reverent as if he was handling not just his grandfather's clue but the old man's faith in what two people could accomplish together.

Inside, another clue waited.

The ring grows closer with each step, / But first you must decide, / Is love worth more than safety? / Is trust worth more than pride? / Seek the place where miners prayed / Before they went below, / Where faith was all they carried / Into darkness down below.

"The mine entrance shrine," Dylan said, her mind already mapping the route. "North boundary, right?"

"About three miles. We could drive, but…" He gestured at the ATVs.

"Race you," she said, already moving.

The ride to the mine was pure adrenaline, weaving through trees, jumping creeks, pushing the machines to their limits while the mountains watched like indulgent grandparents. Dylan won by half a length, pulling up to the sealed mine entrance breathless and triumphant.

The shrine stood beside the sealed mine—a small stone structure where miners had once prayed for safe return from the earth's dark belly. Years of Montana winters had shifted the ground around it, leaving the approach treacherous with loose scree and erosion channels that weren't visible until you were almost on them.

"Careful," Aidan warned, but Dylan was already moving toward the shrine, eager to find the next clue.

The rocks shifted under her boot—a grinding sound like bones breaking. The entire slope seemed to tilt, and suddenly she was sliding toward the mine's sealed entrance where rusted bars covered a darkness that seemed to breathe cold air.

Aidan's hand caught her arm, hauling her back with enough force that they both stumbled away from the unstable edge. They landed hard on solid ground, Dylan's heart hammering against her ribs.

"The whole hillside's been undermined," he said, his voice tight. "Grandda must have come from the other direction."

They circled around, finding a deer path that led to the shrine from above. The structure itself was solid—stone and mortar that had weathered a century of storms—but the ground around the old mine was honeycombed with collapsed tunnels, waiting to swallow the unwary.

"This is why they sealed it," Aidan said. "Kids used to dare each other to go inside before the county put those bars up. Duncan almost fell through a false floor when he was twelve."

Inside the shrine, they found another compartment, another piece of Patrick's elaborate puzzle.

Five stones you've turned, five truths you've learned, / The journey nears its end, / But one more challenge waits for those / Who dare to comprehend. / The highest point, where eagles soar, / Where earth and heaven meet, / There lies the treasure that you seek, / But first, make love complete.

"Eagle's Point," Dylan breathed. "The highest point on O'Hara land."

"Three-hour climb. We'd never make it back before dark."

"Next Saturday then. The final clue."

As they drove back toward the ranch, the sun beginning its descent behind mountains that looked painted by someone in love with drama, Dylan felt the weight of approaching endings—the treasure hunt, the excuse to spend Saturdays with Aidan.

"Let me take you to dinner," Aidan said as they reached the ranch house. "In town."

The invitation hung between them like morning mist over the lake—delicate, beautiful, ready to evaporate at the wrong word.

The warmth that spread through her chest had nothing to do with the afternoon sun. "The Lampstand?"

"Where else? Might as well give the town front-row seats to our lives."

They drove to town as evening painted the valley in shades of amethyst and gold, that mountain twilight that made everything look like it existed in a fairy tale where endings hadn't been written yet. The Lampstand glowed against Main Street like a promise of warmth and witnesses, and Aidan found parking in the lot in front of Hank's construction office.

They walked hand in hand across the street toward Main, where in just a couple of weeks there would be a giant Christmas tree sitting in the center of the *X* that formed downtown. They were already prepping the area for the skating rink, and it would be full of skaters before too long.

Saturday night had filled the restaurant with locals and tourists, the dining room humming with conversation layered like harmonies. Heads turned as they entered together—not unusual for Aidan, who drew attention like flowers drew photographers, but different because his hand rested on Dylan's lower back with unmistakable intention.

Simone seated them in the same booth they'd had the last time. They'd barely ordered when Dylan spotted her—Victoria at the bar, elegant as winter moonlight, a glass of white wine catching the light like captured stars. She wasn't alone—Judge Harrison's wife provided audience for what looked like casual conversation but felt like reconnaissance.

"She's here," Dylan said quietly.

"I know. I saw her when we walked in."

"And you still wanted to eat here?"

"Of course. This is our town. She's the visitor

here, and I'm not going to walk on eggshells trying to avoid her. Besides, you and I have been inseparable for weeks. I think the town knows what's going on between us and that my intentions are pretty clear."

"Hmm," she said, for lack of anything better.

"You have the most incredible eyes," he said, taking her hand. "I've never seen a color like them."

"My mother's eyes," Dylan said softly. "I think it made my dad sad to look at me. I've seen pictures of her. I look like her."

"You look like you," Aidan said. "And you're the most beautiful woman I've ever seen."

She snorted out a laugh at that. "Yeah, right. Especially when I'm covered in grease and grime."

"Honey, that just means you don't know men at all," he said, sitting back with a grin. "I have to catch my breath every time I see you put on those coveralls and cover your hair with that ugly cap."

Her mouth went dry as a bone, and she had trouble swallowing. There was a look in his eyes that was heat and something else she couldn't quite put her finger on. She'd loved him these last five years, dreamed of him—of them together— but she'd kept those feelings in check, understanding they could never come to fruition. But somewhere deep inside her was a spark of hope, a heat that had started as an ember and was fanning into something all consuming. She knew whatever her own gaze held echoed his own, and she would have given anything to be alone with him so the world wasn't intruding on this moment.

Her voice was low and husky when she was finally able to speak. "Maybe you're just weird."

"Maybe so," he said. "I figure there's a reason no other woman has stuck before now. It's just because there's no one like you."

Their food arrived, and they talked about safe things while dancing around dangerous ones—the restoration shop's progress, the weather forecast for next Saturday's climb, how he wanted to kiss her in the moonlight while the light danced behind their eyelids.

Dylan had been so lost in the conversation, in the moment, that she'd completely forgotten Victoria was there until she showed up at their table, breaking the spell of their private bubble. She felt more than saw heads turn their direction.

"Aidan, Dylan," Victoria said with a smile that belonged in a museum of practiced expressions. "I wanted to stop by before I left."

Dylan's hand froze halfway to her water glass. The confidence she'd felt moments ago—the glow from Aidan's attention, the warmth of their dinner—evaporated like steam off hot metal. She was suddenly, acutely aware of every pair of eyes in the restaurant turning their way.

"Victoria." Aidan's voice was carefully neutral, his body language closing off in a way that made something in Dylan's chest tighten with anxiety rather than relief.

"I hope I'm not interrupting." Victoria's gaze swept over their table—the half-eaten meals, the wine glasses, the breadstick Dylan had been reaching for—cataloging everything with the precision of someone inventorying what used to be hers. "I just saw you both here and wanted to properly apologize for the other day at the garage. I was caught off guard."

"It's fine," Dylan said, though her voice came out smaller than she intended.

But Victoria didn't leave. Instead, she gestured to the empty chair with elegant certainty. "Do you mind if I sit for just a moment? I feel terrible about how I came across."

Dylan wanted to object, to say they did mind, but the words stuck somewhere between her heart and her mouth. Around them, she could feel the restaurant's attention like heat on her skin. Everyone was watching. Everyone would be talking about this tomorrow. And Victoria had already claimed the chair before either of them could respond, settling in with the grace of someone who'd never been told no.

"I've been thinking about our brief meeting," Victoria said, looking between them with something that seemed like warmth but felt calculated. "And I realized I was rude. I was just so surprised to see..." she paused delicately, "...how much things had changed at the garage."

"Seven years is a long time," Aidan said evenly.

Victoria's laugh was practiced perfection. "It really is. Do you remember that spring when we drove to Charleston? It feels like yesterday and forever ago all at once." She turned to Dylan with a smile that didn't quite reach her eyes. "Aidan and I got caught in the most ridiculous rainstorm. We ended up dancing in the street like idiots while tourists took pictures."

Dylan felt herself shrinking into her chair. She'd never danced with Aidan in the rain. Never taken spontaneous trips to Charleston. Never been part of the memories that shaped him.

"Or that Christmas at Daddy's estate," Victoria continued, her voice rich with nostalgia. "Your whole family came. It was magical—the house all decorated, the quartet playing in the ballroom. I ran into your mother in the city last year, and she said it was still one of her favorite holidays."

Dylan's stomach clenched. Of course Aidan's mother would remember Christmas parties at estates. Dylan had shared plenty of O'Hara family holidays, but they'd been casual affairs—potlucks and chaos and laughter in the farmhouse kitchen. Not quartets in ballrooms. Not the kind of elegant celebration that Victoria could host, that Victoria's world demanded.

"Victoria—" Aidan started, but she smoothly continued.

"I know, I know. I'm being nostalgic." Victoria leaned forward, and there was something almost kind in her expression that somehow made it worse. "Dylan, I've heard such wonderful things about you since I've been back. The whole town seems impressed with your restoration work. It's quite an achievement, building a reputation like that."

The compliment should have felt good, but delivered in Victoria's patrician voice, it sounded like someone praising a pet for a clever trick.

"Thank you," Dylan managed.

"I have to admit," Victoria said, her gaze sliding between them, "I'm curious how this all came about. You and Aidan working together, I mean. It's such an unlikely pairing." She smiled at Aidan with familiar warmth. "You always said you'd never mix business with pleasure. Remember? After that disaster with the accounting firm in Denver?"

Dylan felt like she was watching a tennis match where she didn't know the rules. Victoria lobbed references and memories over the net, each one landing with casual precision, reminding everyone—especially Dylan—of just how much history she and Aidan shared.

"That was a long time ago," Aidan said, but his voice had lost some of its earlier warmth.

"True. But some things don't change." Victoria's eyes found his with unmistakable meaning. "You still have that tell when you're uncomfortable—that thing you do with your jaw. You're doing it right now."

She was right. Dylan could see it—the slight tension in Aidan's jaw that she'd noticed at the garage but hadn't known was a tell. Victoria knew these things. Victoria had catalogued years of his expressions, his habits, the small truths that Dylan was only beginning to learn.

"We really should let you finish your dinner," Victoria said, glancing at their cooling food with practiced sympathy. "I just wanted to clear the air. No hard feelings about the other day?" She directed this at Dylan, and it was phrased as a question but felt like a statement of dominance.

"Of course not," Dylan said, because what else could she say with the entire restaurant listening?

Victoria stood with fluid grace. "Wonderful. Aidan, we should catch up properly while I'm in town. I'm helping Daddy with some business matters, and I'd love your perspective. You always had such a brilliant mind for these things." She pulled out a business card—of course she had business cards—and placed it on the table. "My cell's on there. Call me."

Then she turned to Dylan one more time. "It's been lovely meeting you properly. I'm sure we'll see more of each other while I'm here." The words were friendly, but something in her eyes said she'd taken Dylan's measure and found her...adequate. Maybe. For now.

After she left, the restaurant slowly resumed its normal rhythm, though Dylan could still feel glances darting their way, conversations being held in lowered voices.

Aidan sat silent for a moment, staring at the business card like it was a snake coiled on the tablecloth.

Dylan couldn't meet his eyes. Inside, she felt like an engine that had been flooded—too much fuel, not enough air, everything choked and uncertain. Victoria had waltzed in and casually demolished any illusion Dylan had that she belonged in Aidan's world. Charleston trips. Christmas parties. Inside jokes and tells and two years of memories that Dylan could never be part of.

"Dylan—" Aidan started.

"She seems nice," Dylan said, the lie tasting like metal on her tongue. "Apologizing like that."

"That wasn't an apology. That was a territorial marking."

Dylan forced herself to look at him. "You danced with her in the rain."

"Seven years ago. In a different life."

"She knows things about you I don't know," Dylan said quietly. "Your mother. Your tells. Your—"

"My past," Aidan interrupted firmly. "She

knows my past, Dylan. But she doesn't know me. Not the me I am now. Not the me I want to be."

He reached for her hand across the table, and Dylan let him take it, though she felt like she was holding on to something that might not be hers to keep.

"That whole performance was about her trying to remind me—and you—of what we had. But what she doesn't understand is that I don't want what we had. It wasn't real. It was me trying to be the person everyone expected me to be."

"She fits in your world," Dylan said. "I don't even know which fork to use half the time."

"I don't care about forks. I care about you. About us. About building something real."

Dylan wanted to believe him. But Victoria's perfume still lingered in the air, expensive and elegant, a reminder of everything Dylan wasn't. And the way the whole restaurant had watched their interaction—she could read their thoughts. Poor Dylan. How can she compete with that?

"Hey," Aidan said softly, squeezing her hand. "Look at me."

She did, and found his gaze steady, almost fierce.

"I moved on from Victoria seven years ago. The only reason I'm even sitting here talking about her is because she won't let the past stay buried. But you—" his voice dropped, intense, "—you're my present. You're who I choose. Please believe that."

Dylan nodded, not trusting her voice. Because she wanted to believe it. She desperately wanted to believe it.

But as they returned to their cooling dinner, making conversation that felt forced after Victoria's interruption, Dylan couldn't shake the feeling that had settled into her bones like a chill—Victoria knew how to belong in Aidan's world. And Dylan was still figuring out if she even wanted to try.

They finished dinner with the quiet unease of people who'd survived a storm only to discover the damage it left behind. As they walked home through November darkness, Main Street quiet except for the whisper of wind through bare branches, Dylan felt something fundamental shift—not in the world but in herself.

At her apartment door, Aidan pulled her close enough that she could feel his heartbeat.

Dylan's mind was still replaying the restaurant—Victoria's practiced laugh, the casual way she'd referenced dancing in the rain, Christmas at the estate, the intimate knowledge of Aidan's tells. *She fits in his world. She knows how to be what he needs.*

"I feel like I've wasted so much time," he whispered, inhaling the scent of her as if he were committing it to memory. "We could have been doing this for five years." He nipped at her lips and then soothed it with a kiss both soft and consuming.

The kiss scattered her thoughts like leaves in wind. For a moment, there was no Victoria, no comparisons, no doubt—just the taste of him, the warmth of his hands on her waist, the way he held her like she was something precious rather than something temporary.

Her breath was shallow and came in pants when he released her what felt like only seconds later. She didn't want him to stop.

"No regrets," she said. "The timing wasn't right."

"And now?" he asked, his green gaze intense on hers.

She swallowed hard, feeling like a coward. She'd dreamed of this for five years, but there'd been a safety in her vision. She'd never expected to stay here. To put down roots. Make this her home. And now that it looked like Laurel Valley was hers, there was a whole new weight bearing down on her of what a real relationship would mean. *What if Victoria's right? What if I can't change patterns that have been ingrained my whole life? What if I'm not enough for him—not sophisticated enough, not polished enough, not permanent enough?*

"And now the timing is right to see what this is," she said. "To see if it's real."

She could tell by the disappointment in his eyes that it wasn't the answer he'd wanted. But it was the only answer she could give.

He kissed her again softly and then took a step back. "Next Saturday. Eagle's Point. We'll search for the final clue."

"The final clue," she agreed, though they both knew they were talking about more than Patrick's treasure hunt.

She unlocked her door and went inside, closing it behind her and then leaning against it. The responsibility of witnessed moments, of public claims and private promises weighed heavy. *Victoria had made everything look so effortless—the belonging, the memories, the way she moved through Aidan's world like she'd been born to it. And here Dylan stood in her paint-splattered apartment, grease still under her fingernails despite scrubbing, wondering if she'd ever be more than the mechanic who got lucky.*

In one week, they'd climb to the highest point

on O'Hara land, find whatever Patrick had hidden there. But would it matter? Would finding some ring change the fact that she didn't know how to dance in the rain, had never hosted elegant Christmas parties, couldn't casually reference shared memories that spanned years instead of months?

But tonight she would treasure the moments—the way his mouth fit against hers, the way his kiss had silenced all her doubts, if only briefly—and not think too much about the future. She'd never had to think about the future before. She'd focus on the restoration shop and the treasure hunt, and anything else could wait.

But somewhere between fixing what was broken and finding what was hidden, she was discovering that the greatest restoration project might be her own heart—learning to trust that some things, some people, some loves were worth the risk of staying still long enough to see what grew. *Even if she wasn't sure she knew how.*

Chapter Ten

THE WEEK FOLLOWING THEIR PUBLIC DINNER unfolded like a flower blooming in time-lapse—each day revealing new colors, new complications, new ways for Dylan to doubt everything while simultaneously feeling more certain than she'd ever been. Laurel Valley had absorbed Aidan's declaration with the efficiency of a small town that treated romance like community property, and Dylan couldn't buy coffee without someone offering relationship advice disguised as pleasantries.

Wednesday afternoon found her at the restoration shop, watching Hank's crew install the final pieces of equipment while her mind churned through Saturday's approaching climb to Eagle's Point. The final clue. The ring. The end of excuses to spend time with Aidan that didn't require admitting that there was more waiting for them.

"Looking good," Hank said, appearing beside her with his tablet and the satisfied expression of someone whose vision had materialized exactly as planned. "Two more weeks and you'll be operational."

"Two weeks." The words tasted like future on her tongue—foreign but not unpleasant.

"Nervous?"

"Terrified."

"Good. Means it matters."

"I've had a dozen calls from potential clients. I'm already booked with projects through the end of next year."

"Good news," Hank said. "You'll be back in the black before you know it."

"No pressure."

Hank studied the space with a contractor's eye, but his voice carried a brother's concern. "Aidan's been different since you agreed to stay. Happier. More…himself, if that makes sense."

"He's always seemed like himself to me."

"No, he's seemed like who he thought he should be. He's got that middle child complex. Always going out of the way to be different than the rest of us. Contrary by nature. When we were kids, if four of us wanted to go fishing, he wanted to go mountain climbing. If we played football, he played baseball. I was worried when Sophie and I got married because I knew that Aidan's hard head would make him stay alone longer just because the rest of us were married."

"Oh, I don't…"

"All I'm saying is that Aidan has never been what he has seemed like to the outside world. He works with his hands in his shop, but he's got a brilliant mind for business. The two of you have a chance to grow something together. And in doing that I think you're going to be the key to finally letting Aidan be who he really is."

Before Dylan could respond, her phone rang.

"Pinnacle Restoration," she answered, thinking it would be another client. Hardly anyone she knew called her. They usually just texted.

"Dylan, this is Victoria," a cool voice said.

"How did you get my number?"

"Sophie gave it to me." Victoria's voice was smooth as aged whiskey. "Before you get angry with her, I told her I wanted to apologize properly for my behavior the first time we met at the garage. I didn't realize you and Aidan were involved."

"Oookay," Dylan said, wondering what was going on. She'd spent most of her time around men growing up and into adulthood. Only in the last few years as she'd spent time with the O'Hara women had she started to learn some of the subtle, and not so subtle, nuances of women. And Victoria was definitely angling for something.

"Could we meet for coffee?"

"Why?" Dylan asked. "My plate is pretty full right now."

Victoria's sigh reached through the receiver, and Dylan felt like a student who asked too many questions.

"Because there are things that need to be said."

Dylan looked at Hank, who was pretending not to eavesdrop. "When?"

"How about now? I'm at Heavenly Delights."

She checked her watch and contemplated. "Give me twenty minutes."

———

Heavenly Delights was nearly empty at three in the afternoon. Victoria had claimed a corner table, looking like she'd been styled for a magazine shoot about elegant women in small towns. Her cream cashmere sweater looked very expensive and wouldn't last a second in the garage.

"I'll be direct," Victoria said as Dylan sat down. "Do you love Aidan?"

The bluntness of it caught Dylan off guard. "I don't think that's any of your business."

"No, it's not." Victoria studied her with cool assessment. "But your hesitation tells me enough. You're not sure."

"Like I said, it's not your business."

"I care about him," she said. "I don't want him to get hurt."

"Like you hurt him?"

"I was foolish," she admitted. "But we were together for two years. I was the one who tamed the tomcat. Before me, he never dated anyone more than a month. Didn't want to be tied down."

"Good for you," Dylan said. "I still don't understand what this has to do with me."

"By your own admission you're not in love with him. At least not all the way. I've learned quite a bit about you since I've been back. Army brat. Raised mostly by her father who was a mechanic. Moved around every couple of years.

Worked by his side until he got too sick and then you bore the brunt of things. And then he died and left you alone, and you've stayed alone. You seem to be comfortable with what you know."

Dylan felt her insides go cold and her hands went clammy. Was her life so easily summed up? "And what do I know?"

"You know you can only rely on yourself. That love isn't permanent, whether through your mother leaving you or through death. I'm surprised you've been in Laurel Valley as long as you have. And I don't expect you to stay. It's hard to change patterns that have been ingrained your whole life."

"I am staying here," she said, though her conviction didn't sound nearly convincing enough. "Aidan and I are partners."

"Aidan is a practical man," Victoria said. "A businessman at heart. He's not emotion driven. Once he sees you're a flight risk he'll come to his senses. And I'll be here for him. Because I do love him. And he'll start to remember the good times we had over those two years, and how aligned our families are, and that we could build an empire together, which is something you and he could never do."

"It sounds like you've got everything planned out," Dylan said, coming to her feet.

"I don't mean to hurt you," she said. "But it's best to know all the cards on the table before you try to play your hand. I still have a chance with Aidan. And I'm going to play my hand."

"I'm not interested in playing your game, so enjoy yourself." Dylan turned and walked out of Heavenly Delights, tamping down the molten embarrassment bubbling up inside of her along with a simmering anger.

"So I haven't made long-term decisions yet," she mumbled under her breath. "Why is everyone in such a hurry? Maybe everyone should just leave me alone."

"You okay?" Raven asked right before Dylan plowed right into her on the sidewalk.

"Oh, God, I'm so sorry," Dylan said as they did a sort of dance to keep from falling. "I didn't see you."

"I expect not," Raven said, the kindness in her eyes almost Dylan's undoing. "You were having quite the conversation. Only one thing can make a woman that angry, and that's an O'Hara man."

"Maybe," she admitted. "Or maybe not. I don't know. I'm so confused. I just had coffee with Victoria."

Raven's smile vanished and she arched a black brow. "Now why'd you go and do a stupid thing like that?"

"Excuse me?" Dylan asked.

Raven put her arm around her shoulders and guided her into the boutique. It smelled of sandalwood and spices, and Dylan couldn't help but notice the rich textures and colors of the clothing displays. She didn't belong in here.

"You got a death wish or something?" Raven asked. "Why in the world would you meet with her?"

"Because she called and said there were things that need to be said."

"Well, whatever she told you, erase them from your mind. Victoria is a barracuda. And she's manipulative."

"She said she still loved Aidan and that because I haven't figured out my feelings yet then that means she still has a chance."

Raven swore, which was so uncharacteristic of her all Dylan could do was stare. "Sorry," she said. "But if you want to know my opinion Victoria never had a chance. We all saw it back when they were together. If you could even really call them together. Anyone with half a brain could see that she was all wrong for Aidan. And Aidan saw it too."

"Then why didn't he break it off with her?"

"Because when things go bad in a relationship, women get domineering and independent, and men go passive. That's just the way of the world. Take it from someone who's been married for a while. It just worked out that Victoria's daddy opened some doors for her to be a shark somewhere else. Believe me, Laurel Valley was glad to see her go. She always acted like more of a tourist than a local. Like everyone here was supposed to serve her."

Dylan snorted out a laugh. "Tell me how you really feel."

Raven grinned. "All I'm saying is don't let whatever seeds she planted in your head take root."

Dylan's phone rang, and she looked down to see Aidan's name pop up. "It's Aidan."

"Lordy, probably everyone in town knows you had coffee with that woman. Better answer quick."

"Hey," Dylan said.

"Hey yourself," he said. "How's the shop looking?"

"Like it's becoming real," she said. "I got another client this morning."

"Which reminds me, now is a good time to start taking applications for help. You'll need a receptionist and a couple of apprentices to help with the restorations. Might be a good idea to call Mr. Otto and see if he had anyone promising who graduated from his shop class last year."

Employees. "Right," she said, wishing she could just go bury herself under a hood somewhere so she didn't have to think about this stuff.

As if Aidan was reading her mind he said, "You'll need help. Especially on the administrative side. You don't want to be stuck doing paperwork when you need to be working on cars."

"Right," she said again. "I'll find someone."

"Good, want to have dinner tonight? My place? I promise to cook something that won't poison you."

"Your place?" She'd never been to his house, only driven past the turnoff on her way to his parent's house.

"Yeah, I thought it'd be nice to have dinner without being under the microscope."

"What time?"

"Seven. I'll text you directions to my house. It's about five miles past the main house, by the lake."

———

That evening, Dylan drove through the O'Hara ranch as twilight painted the valley in shades of lavender and gold. The private road wound like a ribbon through their kingdom, past the main farmhouse where windows bloomed with amber light—each pane a promise of gathered family, of voices raised in laughter and argument, of the kind of belonging that had roots centuries deep.

She continued deeper into the property, where the land opened its arms to embrace the separate homes the brothers had carved from their inheritance. Up here, the road climbed toward Aidan's house, perched on a rise like a hawk's nest overlooking the lake. Built of honey-colored logs and weathered stone, it seemed less constructed than conjured—as if the mountain itself had dreamed of shelter and made it manifest in wood and glass. Windows faced west to catch the last light, turning the peaks into a cathedral of shadow and flame.

He was waiting on the porch for her.

"It's beautiful here," she said, awe and wonder

coloring her voice. "Why would you ever want to leave?"

"Some days it's harder to come into work than others," he said, handing her a glass of wine as she climbed the steps.

The inside revealed itself like a confession—all Aidan, every surface and corner speaking his language. Leather furniture in shades of cognac and chocolate invited rather than impressed, worn soft in the places where he habitually settled. Bookshelves climbed the walls like ivy, heavy with the democratic chaos of a real reader—repair manuals keeping company with dog-eared mysteries, technical diagrams pressed against poetry he'd probably never admit to owning.

The massive stone fireplace commanded the room like an ancient altar, flames painting shadows that danced across pine beams aged to honey. But it was the windows that stole her breath—floor-to-ceiling expanses that transformed the mountains into living art, each peak and valley framed like a masterpiece that changed its mood with the light. This wasn't the careless space of a man marking time until something better came along. This was a home built on the bedrock of intention, every beam and stone a declaration of permanence.

"Kitchen's through here," he said, and she followed him into a space that married rustic bones with modern comfort—copper pots hanging like bells from wrought iron, granite counters that gleamed like dark water, appliances that whispered efficiency beneath their farmhouse façades.

"Fair warning—I'm making venison stew. Duncan got a deer last week. And my mother gave me the recipe. I figure if I can take an engine apart I can follow a recipe."

"It smells amazing." The words came out steadier than she felt.

She perched on a stool at the island, an uninvited ache blooming in her chest as she watched him move through his kitchen with easy competence She didn't believe for a second that he didn't know his way around a kitchen well. The sleeves of his henley were pushed up to reveal forearms that had earned their strength, the firelight from the next room painting gold across his shoulders as he stirred something that smelled like comfort and home and all the things she'd taught herself not to want.

This domestic tableau—Aidan cooking dinner while November pressed its face against the windows, the house settling into evening like a sigh—it was everything she'd never allowed herself to imagine. And that was precisely what made it dangerous.

"Victoria came to see me today," she said, needing it out in the open.

His stirring paused. "I might have heard that somewhere. I was wondering if you'd bring it up."

"She told me she's not giving you up without a fight."

Aidan turned to face her fully. "I don't think she's got anything to hold on to, so I'm not sure who she plans to fight. Maybe I'll sic Raven on her. Raven never liked her. And I bet she's got a mean right hook."

"I don't like being manipulated," she said.

"I can't blame you," Aidan said. "Nobody does."

"Then why do I feel this pressure, no matter which direction I turn? Is your grandfather's treasure hunt real? Or is it another form of manipulation?"

He went very still. "What do you mean?"

"This whole thing—the riddles, the hunt, finding someone to search with. What aren't you telling me?"

He set down the ladle, rubbing the back of his neck in that gesture she'd learned meant he was choosing words thoughtfully. "You're right. There's more to the hunt than I've said."

Dylan's stomach tightened. "Tell me."

"My grandfather's letter—the one that started all this. He didn't just hide the ring for fun. He hid it specifically for…" He paused, then pulled out his wallet, removing a worn piece of paper. "Here. Read it yourself."

Dylan took the letter with hands that weren't quite steady.

My dear boy—and I know it's you, Aidan. You got my looks and my charm, which means you've got my weakness too. You think life's a dance where you never have to pick a partner for more than one song.

By now, they've shown you the ring. It's a fine ring, and it's served the family well. But here's the truth of it, boy—that's not the real ring.

The real claddagh ring, the one blessed by a priest in Galway before the hunger took half of Ireland, is hidden. I've left it somewhere on this land, along with clues to find it. Why? Because nothing worth having comes easy, and love least of all.

You want to know the secret of the O'Haras? It's not charm or looks or the gift of the gab. It's knowing how to work for something. How to earn it. Your grandmother made me prove myself seven times before she'd be my wife.

Find the ring, boy. But more than that, find someone

worth giving it to. Someone who'll make you want to stop dancing and finally learn to stand still.

PS. Don't let your brothers help. They mean well, but this is your adventure. Find someone clever, with brains and heart. And for the love of all that's holy, find someone who can't be charmed by that smile of yours.

Dylan set down the letter, her mind spinning, but Aidan was already moving toward the stove. "Let's eat while it's hot," he said quietly. "Then we can talk through whatever you're thinking."

They sat across from each other at his dining table, the stew rich and warming between them, but Dylan found herself studying his face in the firelight. Victoria's words circled like vultures overhead, picking at the tender places where hope had started to take root. The domesticity of it—the way he'd ladled the stew into bowls his mother had probably given him, the way he'd set out cloth napkins instead of paper—felt simultaneously perfect and suspect.

"The last unmarried O'Hara," she said finally, setting down her spoon. "This whole hunt was about finding you a wife?"

"No," Aidan said quickly, though his own appetite seemed to have fled. "It was about making me work for something. Making me understand that love isn't easy or convenient or—"

"So I'm what? A means to an end? The clever one who helps you get your inheritance?" The words tasted bitter, like medicine she didn't want to swallow but knew she needed.

"Dylan, no. That's not—"

She pushed back from the table, needing distance from the golden circle of lamplight that made everything feel too intimate, too real. "You asked me to help you that first Saturday. Was it because you actually wanted me, or because you were fulfilling some family prophecy?"

"Both. Neither. I don't know." He stood too, the space between them crackling with tension. "Dylan, please. Yes, the letter made me think of you. But not because I was following instructions. Because when he described someone clever with brains and heart, someone who couldn't be charmed, you were the only person I could picture."

"How convenient that your employee fit the description." The words came out sharper than she'd intended, each one a small blade thrown with precision.

"Stop it. You know it's more than that."

But did she? Dylan felt the old familiar panic rising—the sensation of standing on shifting ground, of discovering that what felt solid was actually just another temporary arrangement. "Do I? Because from where I'm standing, it looks like you needed someone to help you find a ring so you could fulfill your grandfather's requirements. And I was available. If Victoria had come to town a few weeks earlier, would it have been her you asked to go on your treasure hunts?"

The hurt that flickered across his features almost made her falter. "Of course not. Is that really what you think? After everything? After five years of—"

"Five years of what? Me working for you? That's all it was until this treasure hunt started."

"That's not true and you know it."

Dylan reached for her coat like a lifeline, needing escape before the words building in her chest could detonate and destroy whatever fragile thing they'd built together. "I need to think."

"Dylan, wait—"

"Saturday's off," she said, hand on the door, autumn air rushing in like cold clarity. "Find someone else to climb your mountain."

She left him standing in his beautiful house with its promise of permanence, drove through the ranch with her vision blurred by tears she refused to acknowledge. The road unwound beneath her tires like all the roads of her childhood—leading away, always away, because staying had never been safe.

Victoria's words echoed in her head like a prophecy she'd been too naïve to see coming. At home, Dylan stood at her window looking out at Main Street, at the life she'd started building without meaning to. The lampposts cast pools of gold on the sidewalks where she'd learned to walk slowly, where she'd discovered that not all conversations had to end in goodbye.

But maybe Victoria was right. Maybe patterns carved in childhood were too deep to escape.

Her phone rang. Aidan's name on the screen like an accusation.

She let it go to voicemail.

Then it rang again. This time she answered, anger overriding the hurt that threatened to hollow her out completely.

"What?"

"You forgot something," he said, his voice rough with emotion she couldn't quite name.

"What did I forget?"

"That I fell for you before I ever read that letter. That I've been falling for you since you walked into my garage and I saw those big violet eyes. Even when you told me my organizational system was chaos, and that you'd only work if country music was on the radio. That my grandfather's hunt didn't create these feelings—it just gave me the courage to acknowledge them."

Dylan sank onto her couch, surrounded by the evidence of roots she'd grown without permission —books she'd bought instead of borrowed, curtains she'd hung, a future she'd dared to imagine. "Aidan—"

"No, listen. Please. I should have told you about the letter from the beginning. But I was scared you'd think exactly what you're thinking now. That this was about the ring, the tradition, the expectation. It's not. It never was."

"Then what is it about?" The question came out smaller than she'd intended, vulnerable as a confession.

"It's about you. It's about the way you see beauty in broken things and make me want to see the world through your eyes. It's about how you've never once looked at me like I was anything other than exactly who I am—not an O'Hara, not the charming one, not the middle one, just Aidan. It's about the fact that I can't imagine my life without you in it, and that has nothing to do with my grandfather or his riddles or that ring sitting on top of a mountain."

Dylan closed her eyes, feeling the weight of five years' worth of careful distance crumbling like a dam she'd built to protect herself from exactly this—from wanting something so much that losing it could break her. "I don't know what to believe."

"You've got things to think about," he said. "Because this isn't all about me. And maybe you don't want to hear this yet, but maybe you're looking for an escape. Maybe you're expecting things to crumble so that gives you the excuse you need to pull up stakes and move on like you always have. It takes courage to stay, Dylan. It takes courage to put down roots. You're not a coward."

"You're right," she said softly, her heart constricting in her chest. "I don't want to hear that yet."

"Then we both have some things to think about this week. Come with me Saturday. Not for the ring, not for the hunt, but for us. Let me show you this isn't about fulfilling some requirement. It's about choosing each other."

The silence stretched between them, filled with everything they'd said and everything they hadn't.

"I'll think about it."

"That's all I can ask."

After they hung up, Dylan sat in her painted apartment, surrounded by the small rebellions against her own nature—the restoration shop that would open in two weeks, the roots she'd started growing in soil she'd never trusted before. The ring waited on Eagle's Point like a question mark against the sky. And somewhere between Victoria's calculated cruelty and Aidan's raw honesty, between the fear that had kept her safe and the hope that might destroy her, Dylan had to decide what she believed.

What she wanted.

Who she was brave enough to become.

Thursday brought no clarity, only the slow torture of Victoria's presence woven through Laurel Valley like a golden thread designed to remind everyone what they'd lost.

Friday afternoon, Dylan's phone rang.

Sophie's cheerful voice greeted her. "First of all, let me apologize. I had no idea that Victoria was going to call you and invite you for coffee. I thought she sincerely wanted to apologize."

"No worries," Dylan said. "Truly. It was very enlightening. It was probably better to go ahead and get it out of the way."

"Good," Sophie said. "Now on to business. Whatever you're thinking about tomorrow, stop overthinking it."

"How do you know I'm overthinking?"

"Because you didn't come to book club last night, you've been avoiding Main Street, and Aidan looks like someone stole his favorite socket wrench."

Despite everything, Dylan felt her mouth twitch. "It's complicated."

"Love always is. But Dylan? That man has been half in love with you for years. The treasure hunt just gave him an excuse to do something about it."

"How can you know that?"

"Because I've watched him watch you. The way he lights up when you walk into a room. The way he finds excuses to be wherever you are. The way he's never seriously dated anyone since you arrived, despite half the valley throwing themselves at him."

After Sophie hung up, Dylan stood in her restoration shop, surrounded by the future she'd carved from nothing but stubbornness and skill.

Tools hung in neat rows like promises she'd made to herself. Project cars waited under white covers like sleeping possibilities.

And for the first time since she'd fled Aidan's house, Dylan allowed herself to remember what it felt like when he looked at her—not like she was convenient or available or the solution to someone else's puzzle, but like she was exactly what he'd been hoping to find.

Saturday morning, she'd climb that mountain.

Not for the ring.

Not for the hunt.

But to find out if love was worth the risk of believing in it.

Chapter Eleven

Saturday morning crept across the O'Hara ranch wearing storm clouds like a warning, the mountains invisible behind gray that pressed down with the weight of winter's first serious threat. Dylan sat in her Charger at the base of the trail that wound up Eagle's Point, watching dawn struggle through the overcast, her hands wrapped around a thermos of coffee she couldn't taste past the knot in her throat.

She'd dressed for weather—thermal base layers under fleece-lined pants, her father's old military surplus jacket over a wool sweater Sophie had insisted she buy last winter, waterproof hiking boots that had seen actual miles. Her knit cap was pulled low over her ears, gloves tucked in her pockets. She looked like someone who understood mountains could kill you with cold as easily as with falling.

She'd almost not come. Had spent the night constructing elaborate excuses—the weather, the restoration shop's pending inspection, the McLaren that needed one final adjustment. But Sophie's words had echoed through her sleepless hours—*That man has been half in love with you for years.*

Headlights cut through the gloom, and Aidan's truck pulled up beside her. Through the rain-spotted glass, she watched him check his reflection in the mirror. Five years she'd been watching him do that. Five years of cataloging his habits like she was writing a manual on Aidan O'Hara, never realizing she was actually writing a love letter.

He climbed out, dressed in similar layers—the expensive technical gear that spoke of someone who'd grown up with mountains as his backyard. The backpack he shouldered looked serious enough for real weather, and she noticed the ice axe strapped to its side.

"I'm glad you came," he said when she joined him at the trailhead, and the relief in his voice made something loosen in her chest.

They stood in the gray morning, both aware this was more than just the final clue. This was the choosing—not just the ring or the riddle, but each other, the future, the possibility of permanence Dylan had spent thirteen years avoiding.

"Weather's turning," Aidan said, studying the sky with the inherited knowledge of someone whose family had been reading Montana weather for five generations. "We could postpone—"

"No." The word came out sharper than intended. "If we don't do this today, I don't know if I'll have the courage again."

Something shifted in his expression—understanding mixing with determination. "Then we climb."

The trail began gently enough, winding through forest that held its breath in the storm-heavy air. Their boots found rhythm on the packed earth, the silence between them full but not uncomfortable. Dylan had expected awkwardness after their confrontation, but instead found something else—a sense of inevitability, like they were walking toward something that had been waiting for them all along.

"Tell me about the ring," she said after they'd been climbing for twenty minutes. "The real one. What makes it worth all this?"

Aidan ducked under a low branch heavy with moisture, holding it aside for her. "Legend says it was blessed by a priest in Galway before the famine. The blessing was specific—that whoever wore it would find love that could survive any storm, any distance, any loss."

"You believe that?"

"I believe my ancestors believed it. And sometimes that's enough—believing in the power of belief."

The trail steepened, forcing conversation to give way to breath. Dylan's legs burned with the familiar ache of effort, her body remembering other mountains, other climbs, always alone. But now Aidan moved just ahead, his presence constant as gravity, occasionally looking back to check her progress with eyes that held worry and something warmer.

An hour in, the forest began to thin, evergreens giving way to alpine meadows dressed in November brown. The wind picked up, carrying the metallic scent of snow, a smell that made primitive parts of the brain whisper about shelter and survival.

"Storm's coming faster than predicted," Aidan said, stopping to pull weather gear from his pack. "We should—"

The first snowflakes interrupted him—fat, heavy flakes that didn't drift so much as plummet, like the sky had suddenly decided to empty its pockets. Within minutes, the world transformed from gray to white, visibility shrinking to mere yards.

"We need to make the peak before this gets worse," Aidan said, having to raise his voice over wind that had gone from whisper to howl. "The cairn where Grandda hid the ring—if we don't find it now, it could be buried until spring."

They pushed upward, the trail becoming treacherous as snow accumulated with shocking speed. Dylan's world narrowed to the placement of each foot, the burn in her lungs, the broad shape of Aidan's back just ahead. The mountain had become something else—not just earth and stone but a living thing that tested with wind and cold and the promise that nature didn't care about human plans or human hearts.

The peak revealed itself suddenly—they crested a rise and there it was, a flat expanse of granite swept clean by wind that seemed to come from all directions at once. The cairn stood at the highest point, a precisely stacked pile of stones that had weathered decades of seasons.

"There," Aidan shouted over the wind.

They fought their way to the cairn together, Dylan holding the flashlight while Aidan, pulling off his gloves for better grip, dismantled stones made slick with snow. She watched his hands redden with cold, saw them shake as he worked each stone free with the patience of someone handling sacred things.

"Got it," he breathed, pulling out a metal box that had been hidden in the cairn's heart.

Inside, wrapped in oilcloth like a covenant against time, lay a wooden box that might have been carved when America was young. The wood was dark with age, worn smooth not by weather but by handling—generations of O'Hara fingers tracing its edges, opening it for christenings and weddings, for all the moments when love required witness. Aidan's hands trembled as he lifted the lid —definitely from emotion now, not cold.

The ring lay on velvet that had once been rich purple but time had gentled to the color of twilight. It seemed to gather what little light filtered through the storm and hold it, the silver warm despite the cold. The claddagh design— two hands cradling a crowned heart—had been worn soft by centuries of wearing, the details gentled but not erased. Around the band, words in Gaelic spiraled like a prayer made metal, the letters so small they seemed more felt than read.

"What does it say?" Dylan asked, leaning close enough that their heads nearly touched.

"*Grá, Dílseacht, Cairdeas,*" Aidan read slowly, his finger tracing the ancient words. "Love, Loyalty, Friendship. But there's more—Tríd an stoirm. Through the storm." His voice caught on the last words. "My God, Dylan. It's like he knew. Like they all knew we'd be standing here in this exact moment."

As if the mountain had been waiting for that recognition, the wind suddenly shrieked with renewed violence, snow going from heavy to horizontal. The world vanished into white chaos, the cairn disappearing though it stood mere feet away.

"We have to get down," Aidan shouted, grabbing Dylan's hand. "Now."

But down had become a theoretical concept. The trail they'd climbed had vanished under snow that was accumulating at an impossible rate. Every direction looked the same—white fury and wind that tried to tear them from the mountain's face.

"The hunting cabin," Aidan said, pulling her against him so she could hear. "Old family shelter. Northeast face, about half a mile down."

They descended by instinct and prayer, Aidan leading with the inherited knowledge of someone whose blood knew these slopes. Dylan trusted his steps, followed his path, her hand in his the only warm thing in a world gone arctic.

The cabin materialized from the storm like salvation—a sturdy structure built by Aidan's great-grandfather for hunting seasons, maintained by each generation since. The door fought them, wind trying to tear it from Aidan's grip, but they tumbled inside, the sudden absence of wind so shocking that Dylan's ears rang with the silence.

"Power of belief, huh?" she gasped, collapsing against the closed door.

Aidan was already moving with practiced efficiency. The cabin was spartan but prepared—a wood stove, stacked wood, emergency supplies that his mother refreshed every summer, two narrow bunks with wool blankets and sleeping bags. This was O'Hara territory, and O'Haras took care of their own, even when their own was just an empty cabin waiting for moments like this.

"We need heat," he said, his hands shaking as

he worked to start a fire in the stove. "Temperature's dropping fast."

Dylan helped, holding kindling while he coaxed flame from matches that didn't want to cooperate with numb fingers. The fire caught, tentative at first, then growing stronger, pushing back the cold that had followed them inside.

As warmth began to creep into the cabin, they took inventory. No cell signal—the mountain blocked everything. The storm showed no signs of lessening. They had shelter, heat, and the emergency supplies Anne refreshed religiously, but they were effectively trapped until weather cleared.

"So much for avoiding the town microscope," Dylan said, pulling off her soaked outer layers.

"They'll send search and rescue when we don't check in." Aidan was doing the same, hanging wet clothes near the stove. "Wyatt knows exactly where this cabin is. We all do. It's practically family legend—Duncan got lost up here when he was seven, found the cabin and stayed put for two days living on beef jerky and melted snow until Dad found him."

They settled on the floor near the stove, sharing an emergency blanket and the surreal intimacy of survival. The ring box sat between them, its contents catching firelight like captured stars.

"Your grandfather planned everything else," Dylan said. "You don't think he somehow planned this?"

Aidan's laugh was warm as summer honey. "Controlling weather would be impressive, even for him. Though knowing Grandda, he probably prayed for whatever would bring truth to the surface."

The storm howled around the cabin like something alive and hungry, but inside, the fire created a bubble of warmth and light. Dylan was acutely aware of Aidan beside her—the heat of him, the way his shoulder pressed against hers, the fact that they were alone in a way they'd never been before.

"I'm sorry," she said quietly. "For running. For assuming the worst. For being so ready to believe this was all manipulation instead of—"

"Instead of what?"

She turned to look at him, finding his face closer than expected, his eyes reflecting firelight like green flames. "Instead of you choosing me. Actually choosing me, not because your grandfather said to find someone clever, but because—"

"Because you make every day better just by being in it. Because watching you work is like watching someone conduct a symphony. Because you look at what's damaged and see the potential for restoration, and you helped me see that in myself too."

"When?" she whispered. "When did you know?"

"There was a morning, maybe three years ago. You were under that horrible woman's Bentley, and you were humming—off-key, completely absorbed. And suddenly you laughed at something, maybe the solution to whatever problem you'd been chasing. And I stood there thinking—I could listen to that laugh for the rest of my life and never get tired of it."

Dylan's heart was attempting escape through her throat. "Aidan—"

"I'm not asking for promises," he said quickly. "We're trapped in a cabin in a blizzard. But Dylan, this ring—it's not just mine to give. It belongs to the family, to the generations that come after. It gets passed to the last bachelor, and he gives it to his bride, and one day their son will search for someone worthy of it. It's bigger than just us."

"That's a lot of pressure."

"That's a lot of history. But history is just people choosing each other, over and over, through everything." He picked up the ring box, turning it so the silver caught the light. "My grandmother wore this for fifty-six years. Through war and peace, children and grandchildren, loss and joy. She wore it while she planted her moon garden and while she buried her firstborn who died in infancy. She wore it until the day she died, and then Grandda kept it safe for the next love story."

"And you think we could be that? That kind of love story?"

"I think we already are. We just haven't admitted it yet."

The wind chose that moment to scream against the cabin walls, rattling the windows like something trying to get in. Dylan shivered despite the warmth.

"We should try to sleep," Aidan said, though his eyes suggested sleep was the furthest thing from his mind. "The bunks are small, but with the sleeping bags—"

"We could share," Dylan heard herself say. "For warmth. Purely practical."

His eyes darkened, but his voice remained steady. "Dylan, I don't think that's—"

"I trust you," she said simply. "And I'm freezing, and those bunks are narrow, and I don't want to be alone tonight while the mountain tries to blow us off its face."

They made a nest of sleeping bags and blankets on one bunk, fully clothed in their dried base layers, curled together like quotation marks around an unspoken truth. Aidan's arm around her waist was careful, respectful, but she could feel the tension in his body, the effort it took to hold still.

"Dylan," he said into the darkness, his breath warm against her neck.

"I know," she whispered. "I know we need to wait. I know you're an honorable man. I know when we take that step, you want it to be right. I just—I needed to be close to you. Is that okay?"

His arm tightened around her, pulling her back against his chest. "It's more than okay. It's perfect. You're perfect."

"I'm not—"

"You are to me." He pressed a kiss to her hair, chaste but somehow more intimate than anything else they'd shared. "Sleep. Tomorrow we'll deal with the town and my mother and all the assumptions. Tonight, just let me hold you."

Dylan closed her eyes, feeling his heartbeat against her back, strong and steady as the mountain itself. Outside, the storm raged like the end of the world, but inside their small shelter, she felt safer than she had in thirteen years.

"The ring," she said sleepily. "We found it."

"We did."

"What happens now?"

"Now we become the next chapter in its story. If you'll have me. If you're ready to stop running."

"I already have," she murmured, drowsing toward dreams. "Stopped running, I mean. I stopped the moment you said the ring was about choosing each other through the storms."

Sleep took her gently, while Aidan lay awake holding her, marveling at the way she fit against him like she'd been designed for this exact space. The ring sat in its box on the small table, patient as it had been for centuries, waiting for the next part of its story to unfold.

Morning came dressed in silence and diamond light. Dylan woke slowly, aware first of warmth, then of Aidan's arm still around her, then of the absolute quiet that meant the storm had passed. She turned in his embrace, finding him already awake, watching her with an expression that made her chest ache.

"Hi," she whispered.

"Hi yourself." He didn't move to kiss her,

though she could see he wanted to. "Storm's over."

"I can hear that."

"They'll be coming for us soon."

"I know."

"The whole town will think—"

"I know that too." She reached up, tracing his jaw with one finger. "I don't care what they think. I care what we know."

"And what do we know?"

"That we chose each other. That we'll keep choosing each other. That your grandfather was right—love is about the reaching for it together."

A distant sound made them both turn—the rhythmic thrum of helicopter rotors growing closer.

"Search and rescue," Aidan said. "Right on time."

They dressed quickly, packing up the cabin with the efficiency of people raised to leave places better than they found them. The ring went into Aidan's pocket, its weight a promise neither of them needed to speak aloud.

The helicopter appeared over the ridge in a glory of morning sun on metal, Wyatt visible in the door with his serious search-and-rescue expression that dissolved into a grin the moment he saw they were safe.

As they climbed aboard, Dylan looked back at the cabin—that small shelter that had held them through the storm, that had given them space to finally say what needed saying. The mountain rose behind it, Eagle's Point crowned with new snow that sparkled like the ring hidden in Aidan's pocket.

"Interesting night?" Wyatt asked with brotherly innocence that fooled no one.

"Shut up and fly," Aidan said, but he was smiling, his hand finding Dylan's as the helicopter lifted them toward home.

Below, the valley spread out like a promise—Laurel Valley dressed in winter white, smoke rising from chimneys, the town preparing for another day of gentle gossip and communal care.

Dylan squeezed Aidan's hand, feeling the future unspool before them like a road through mountains—sometimes steep, sometimes treacherous, but always leading home.

To each other.

To the life they'd build together.

To love that could weather any storm.

Chapter Twelve

THE HELICOPTER DESCENDED THROUGH MORNING light that turned the snow-covered valley into something from a snow globe—pristine, perfect, impossibly bright after the storm's darkness. Dylan could see the crowd gathered in the town square, their faces turned skyward with the universal expression of small towns when their own go missing—relief mixed with rabid curiosity about what happened while they were gone.

"Brace yourself," Wyatt said over the headset, but his grin suggested he was enjoying this far too much. "Mom mobilized half the town when you didn't check in last night. She's got breakfast waiting at The Lampstand for what looks like everyone we've ever met."

The landing zone had been cleared in the park, and as they touched down, Dylan could see the full scope of what awaited them. Anne O'Hara stood at the front like a general who'd won her war, her face shifting from maternal concern to something that looked dangerously close to satisfaction. Behind her, Sophie and Raven flanked her, their expressions suggesting they'd already written several versions of what had happened in that cabin.

The moment the rotors began to slow, Anne was moving, reaching them before they'd even properly disembarked.

"Thank God," she breathed, pulling Aidan into a hug that could have cracked ribs, then surprising Dylan by embracing her with equal fervor. "When the storm came in so fast, and then you didn't answer your phones—"

"We're fine, Mom," Aidan said, his arm settling around Dylan's shoulders with a naturalness that sent whispers rippling through the crowd. "The hunting cabin saved us."

"The cabin," Anne repeated, and something in her tone made Dylan look at her sharply. The older woman's blue eyes held a gleam that had probably been responsible for five marriages and counting. "Of course. Your grandfather always said that cabin would serve its purpose when the time was right."

"Mom," Aidan warned, but Anne had already shifted into full maternal orchestration mode.

"You must be freezing. Both of you. Sophie, tell Simone we need the private dining room. Raven, call Colt, have him meet us there—"

"Mom, he's your son, not our doctor," Aidan protested. "We don't need medical attention because we got cold."

"You spent the night in a storm that dropped two feet of snow," Anne countered with the authority of someone who'd raised five boys and knew exactly how to override objections. "You'll see your brother, you'll eat hot food, and then you'll tell us everything."

The "everything" came loaded with enough subtext to sink a ship.

"Anne," Mick O'Hara's voice cut through the chaos with quiet authority. He'd approached more slowly, his weathered face revealing relief and something else—a knowing look that he shared with his son over Dylan's head. "Let them breathe. They're safe. That's what matters."

But Laurel Valley had its own momentum when drama presented itself, and Dylan found herself swept along in a tide of concerned citizens toward The Lampstand. She caught glimpses of familiar faces—Rose from the bakery pressing a bag of warm pastries into her hands, Bernie Watson nodding approval like they'd passed some test, Mrs. Whitfield from the historical society watching with the satisfaction of someone who'd seen this coming five years ago.

The Lampstand's private dining room had been transformed into command central. Colt waited with his medical bag, Simone had laid out enough breakfast food to feed the town, and what appeared to be the entire O'Hara clan had materialized with the efficiency of people who understood that family drama required full attendance.

"Sit," Anne commanded, and Dylan found herself obeying before she could form a protest.

Colt's examination was perfunctory, his hands gentle as he checked for signs of hypothermia or frostbite while rolling his eyes at his mother's hovering. "They're fine, Mom. Though I'm curious how you managed to stay so warm in that cabin with just the wood stove."

The question hung in the air like a lit fuse. Dylan felt heat climb her neck that had nothing to do with the coffee Simone had placed in front of her.

"We shared body heat," Aidan said calmly, meeting his brother's gaze directly. "For survival."

"Survival," Duncan repeated from his perch by the window, his artist's eye taking in every detail of their body language. "Is that what we're calling it?"

"We're calling it two people not freezing to death," Dylan said, finding her voice and the courage that came with it. "Though I'm sure the town has already written a much more interesting story."

"Several versions, actually," Sophie admitted with characteristic honesty. "Bernie Watson has you engaged. Rose thinks you're already secretly married. And Mrs. Johannson is convinced this was all a plot to trap Aidan into marriage."

Dylan nearly choked on her coffee.

"Speaking of marriage," Hank said with the subtlety of a sledgehammer, "When a man spends the night with a woman, even in survival situations, there are certain expectations—"

"Hank," Aidan warned.

"I'm just saying," Hank continued, "that our grandfather would have expected you to make an honest woman out of her."

"She's already an honest woman," Aidan said, his jaw tightening.

"You know what he means," Duncan chimed in, enjoying himself far too much. "The family ring, a night alone, the whole town watching—seems like the universe is trying to tell you something."

"The universe needs to mind its own business," Dylan muttered, but she was fighting a smile.

"Did you at least find the ring?" Wyatt asked, attempting to shift the conversation to safer ground.

The room went silent with sudden completeness. Aidan reached into his pocket, pulling out the box that had survived centuries and storms and the weight of expectation.

When he opened it, the collective intake of breath sounded like wind through pines. The ring caught the morning light streaming through windows, silver warming to gold, the ancient claddagh design seeming to pulse with life.

"My God," Anne breathed, her hand going to her heart. "I haven't seen it since your grandmother wore it." Her eyes filled with tears that she didn't try to hide. "She'd be so happy, Aidan. She always said you'd know when the time was right."

"The time for what?" Dylan asked, though she suspected she knew.

"For the last O'Hara bachelor to stop being a bachelor," Colt said with medical precision. "It's practically a biological imperative at this point. We're all married. Aidan's the last holdout."

"No pressure though," Wyatt added with a grin that suggested the opposite.

"You could propose right now," Sophie suggested helpfully.

"For heaven's sake," Aidan said, but Dylan noticed his hand had moved to cover the ring box protectively.

"It would solve the scandal," Raven mused, her elegant features arranged in false innocence. "You did spend the night together. Unchaperoned. In a cabin. During a blizzard. Very romantic, but also very—"

"Very none of anyone's business," Dylan finished, but her heart was racing because everyone in the room was looking at them with expectation that felt like gravity, pulling them toward something inevitable. "And we're adults. In the twenty-first century. It's not 1892. No need for a shotgun wedding."

"It's Laurel Valley," Sophie said as if that explained everything.

"Though if you were engaged," Anne went on as if no one else had spoken, "it would certainly quiet any inappropriate speculation about last night."

"Mom," all five brothers said in unison.

But Anne O'Hara hadn't raised five boys without learning how to read the unspoken, and her gaze found Dylan's with surprising directness. "I'm not trying to pressure anyone. I'm just saying that sometimes storms bring clarity. Sometimes being forced to stop running and just…be still with someone…shows you what's been true all along."

The words hit Dylan like physical things, each one finding its mark. She'd been running for thirteen years. Last night, trapped in that cabin with nowhere to run, she'd finally understood what staying might feel like.

"Speaking of storms," Mick said quietly. "There's another one coming midweek. Supposed to be worse than last night's."

"Better get the important things done before then," Duncan said with studied casualness. "You know, in case anyone gets trapped again."

Dylan looked around the table at these people who'd become family without her quite noticing—the brothers who teased but would defend, the wives who'd pulled her into their circle, the parents who'd made space for her at their table before she'd even known she wanted it.

Then she looked at Aidan, who was watching her with those green eyes that had undone her from the beginning, his expression a mixture of exasperation and something deeper, warmer, more permanent.

"Are you proposing?" she asked him directly.

The room went still as held breath.

Aidan studied her for a long moment, then his mouth curved in that slow smile that had been undermining her defenses for five years. "Would you like me to?"

"I asked you first."

"So you did." He stood, pulling her to her feet with him, the ring box still in his hand. Around them, his family leaned forward like flowers toward sun. "Dylan Flanagan, would you like me to propose to you in front of my entire meddling family and half the town, or would you prefer something more private?"

"I'd prefer honesty," she said, her voice steadier than her pulse. "Are you asking because they expect it, or because you want to?"

"I'm asking," he said, his free hand coming up to frame her face with a tenderness that made her chest ache, "because you captivated my attention when you walked into my garage five years ago looking for a job. Because knowing you, being friends with you, captured my heart. And because loving you has been an honor I'll cherish for the rest of our lives."

"Wow," she said, hearing sniffles from the onlookers. Tears streamed down her own cheeks. When was the last time she'd cried? She couldn't remember. But she could trust Aidan with her heart.

He dropped to one knee right there in The Lampstand's private dining room, with his entire family as witness. "I'm going to do this properly."

He opened the ring box, the ancient silver catching light like captured stars.

"This ring has been in my family for three hundred years. It's seen famine and feast, crossings and arrivals, love and loss and love again. It's not just a ring—it's a promise that some things endure. That some loves are worth the storms. That some people are worth staying for, worth building with, worth choosing over and over again."

Dylan's vision blurred, but she didn't need to see clearly to know what her answer was. She'd known it last night in the cabin. Known it this morning when she'd woken in his arms. Maybe known it five years ago when she'd reorganized his disaster of an office and he'd laughed instead of getting angry.

"I need you to know," she said, her voice carrying clear despite the tears, "that I'm not saying yes because we got caught in a storm, or because people think I'm a fallen woman, or because your family expects it. I'm saying yes because you're the reason I stopped running. Because you made Laurel Valley feel like home. Because I love you, and I've been loving you so long I forgot what it felt like not to."

"Is that a yes?" he asked, though his grin suggested he knew.

"Yes, Aidan O'Hara. Yes to the ring, yes to your overwhelming family, yes to staying, yes to all of it."

He slipped the ring onto her finger, the metal warm as a blessing, fitting perfectly as if it had been waiting for her all along. Then he was standing, pulling her into a kiss that would probably be talked about in Laurel Valley for the next fifty years—the kind of kiss that made married couples remember their own beginnings and single people believe in possibilities.

When they finally broke apart, the room erupted. Anne was crying openly, Mick was shaking Aidan's hand with the vigor of a man who'd been waiting for this moment, and the brothers were engaging in the kind of cheerful chaos that suggested celebrations and bachelor party planning.

"I call best man," Wyatt announced.

"You can't call it," Duncan protested. "It should be the oldest—"

"It should be whoever hasn't been best man yet," Colt interjected.

"Slow down," Dylan laughed, but she was crying too, her hand finding Aidan's like an anchor. "We just got engaged thirty seconds ago."

"In this family, that's thirty seconds too long to wait for wedding planning," Sophie said, hugging her tightly. "Welcome to the O'Hara chaos, officially."

"Wouldn't a spring wedding be lovely," Anne said. "The flowers are beautiful then."

"I was thinking next week," Dylan said, winking at Aidan. "Before the storm comes."

"You heard the woman," Aidan said, making his brothers laugh.

"Ten days until the restoration shop opens," Dylan said, looking up at Aidan. "Think we can plan a wedding and launch a business at the same time?"

"We can do anything," he said, his arm around her waist, the ring on her finger catching light with every movement. "We found a centuries-old ring in a freak snowstorm. Everything else is easy."

But it wasn't about easy, Dylan thought as she looked around the room at these people who'd become hers. It was about choosing the hard things—the staying, the trusting, the building something that would last longer than fear.

The storm had brought clarity, just as Anne had said. But the real clarity had come in the quiet after—in the warmth of being held, in the certainty of being chosen, in the courage to say yes to a future that terrified and thrilled her in equal measure.

Victoria Pemberton chose that moment to appear in the doorway, elegant even at eight in the morning, her expression carefully composed. She took in the scene—Dylan's tear-stained face, the ring catching light on her finger, Aidan's protective arm around her, the family surrounding them like a living wall.

"I heard the helicopter," she said quietly. "I wanted to make sure everyone was all right."

"We're perfect," Aidan said, and the simple certainty in his voice made Victoria's composure flicker.

Her gaze found the ring on Dylan's finger, and something shifted in her expression—surprise, maybe, or recognition of a battle that had been lost before it was even fought.

"Congratulations," she said, and to her credit, it sounded genuine. "It's a beautiful ring. A beautiful story."

"Thank you," Dylan said, meaning it. This woman had loved Aidan once, or thought she had. That meant she had good taste, even if she'd thrown it away for ambition.

"My father's doing better," Victoria said, already retreating. "We'll be heading back to New York tomorrow. If the two of you are ever looking for investors, the door is always open. You both do exceptional work."

"Thank you," Dylan said.

After she left, the room seemed to exhale.

"Well," Anne said with satisfaction. "We need to start wedding planning. I accept your challenge of a week."

As the morning dissolved into laughter and planning and the cheerful chaos of family, Dylan found herself standing at the window, looking out at Main Street where life was returning to normal after the storm. The snow sparkled in morning sun, making everything look new, transformed, possible.

Aidan came up behind her, his arms wrapping around her waist, his chin resting on her shoulder. "Any regrets?"

"None," she said, turning the ring on her finger, feeling the weight of centuries, the promise of tomorrow. "You?"

"Only that it took us five years to get here."

"We got here at exactly the right time," she said, leaning back into his warmth. "Any sooner and I might have run.

"We could elope," he suggested. "Drive to Vegas, get married by Elvis, send everyone postcards."

"Your family would hunt us down. I can wait a week if you can."

He sighed. "Pure torture. I didn't get a wink of sleep last night holding you in my arms."

"Funny," she said, burrowing into his chest. "I slept like a baby. Safe and protected."

They stood together watching the town wake up properly, watching neighbors emerge to clear snow and exchange gossip about the helicopter rescue and what it might mean. By noon, everyone would know. By evening, it would be settled fact—Dylan Flanagan and Aidan O'Hara, engaged after a dramatic storm rescue, the ring found, the last bachelor claimed, another chapter in Laurel Valley's love stories.

"I love you," Aidan said against her ear. "I've loved you since you walked into my life and started fixing things I didn't even know were broken."

"I love you too," she replied.

"Our business, our family, our future," he said. "We make a heck of a team."

Our. Such a small word to carry so much weight. But as Dylan stood there in his arms, wearing a ring that had crossed oceans and centuries to find its way to her finger, surrounded by family that had chosen her before she'd known she wanted to be chosen, she understood that some weights weren't burdens.

Some weights were anchors, keeping you steady in storms, keeping you moored to what mattered. Dylan had spent thirteen years running from the possibility of loss.

Now, she was ready to stand still long enough to see what grew.

December snow fell on the O'Hara ranch with the steady devotion of a lover's promise, transforming the Montana landscape into something softer, more forgiving than the harsh land that had greeted Thomas and Seamus when they'd first claimed this valley in 1847. Through the farmhouse kitchen window, Dylan O'Hara watched winter paint the world white while flour dusted her hands like a blessing.

Two years since she'd married Aidan in a whirlwind week that still had the town talking. Two years since Pinnacle Restoration had opened its doors, fulfilling dreams she'd carried like stones in her pockets for thirteen years of running. Now Maggie squirmed in her arms—fourteen months of green-eyed determination wrapped in her father's charm and her mother's iron will.

The claddagh ring caught the light as Dylan shifted the baby—an O'Hara family treasure, centuries old, blessed in Galway before the famine sent desperate souls across the Atlantic. It had witnessed every storm, every joy, every loss that had shaped this family from Irish rebels to Montana royalty.

"She's going to rule the world, that one," Anne said, appearing with the timing of a woman who'd orchestrated decades of family gatherings in this kitchen. Her red hair, silver threaded now but still glorious, caught the light as she moved through her domain. "Just like her father at that age. Always into everything."

Through the window, the sycamore trees stood skeletal against the sky, their bony branches framing Twin Peaks in the distance—those mountains that had watched over every O'Hara triumph and heartbreak since the beginning.

The kitchen door—never locked because O'Haras believed in open doors and full hearts— burst open with winter wind and children's laughter. Harrison tumbled through first, five years of barely contained energy, with older sister Mary

Catherine behind him, rolling her eyes at his immaturity.

"The road's getting interesting," Duncan announced, following his children inside, snow melting in his black hair. Hattie moved through the doorway with late pregnancy's awkward grace, one hand protective over the child who'd arrive within the next month.

"That's everyone except Colt," Anne said, checking her mental roster. "He's always late these days."

"Doctor's hours," Mick said from the doorway of his office, definitely not smelling of cigar smoke, definitely not having just used his portable fan. His blue eyes—that brilliant Irish blue—twinkled with the mischief of a man who'd been getting away with things for sixty years.

Within the hour, the farmhouse filled with O'Haras like water finding its level. Wyatt and Raven with their twins, Patrick and Seamus, chaos in motion. Sophie and Hank with three-year-old Liam and fifteen-month-old Grace, Sophie glowing with the beginnings of a new pregnancy. And finally Colt and Zoe, her writer's schedule making them perpetually late, their three-year-old twins and baby Eleanor completing the set.

Chewy padded in behind them, more dignified than he had been in his youth.

"Complete chaos out there," Colt announced cheerfully. "Roads are getting bad."

"Wouldn't be Christmas without a storm," Mick said with satisfaction.

When Anne rang Margaret O'Hara's bell—silver worn smooth by decades—everyone moved toward the dining room with the ease of tradition. It took the usual negotiations to get everyone seated, high chairs multiplying like miracles, children vibrating with Christmas Eve energy.

Mick stood at the head of the table, and when he raised his weathered hands, even the babies stilled. The candlelight flickered across his face as he began the ritual that anchored them all.

"Before we feast," he said, his voice carrying that Irish lilt that emerged for moments that mattered, "we remember."

The room held its breath, even the children sensing the weight of history.

"We remember those brothers who fled Ireland with nothing but determination. Who found this valley and planted the stake here when they could have kept running. Who built with hands that bled and backs that broke but hearts that wouldn't quit."

His gaze traveled to each son's wife, and Dylan felt herself seen, claimed, woven into a story that had started centuries before her birth.

"We remember that O'Haras have always been saved by the women brave enough to take them on. Raven, who kept faith through secrets and storm. Zoe, who literally got knocked into love and decided the concussion was worth keeping. Hattie, who chose to trust again when trust seemed impossible. Sophie, who built beauty from ashes. And Dylan…"

The pause stretched like honey, sweet and golden.

"Dylan, who stopped running long enough to restore not just cars but the heart of my son who'd forgotten what it meant to stand still."

He raised his glass, wine catching light like liquid rubies.

"To those who came before, who planted seeds in foreign soil. To those who come after, who will continue the family name. To the storms that test us and the love that sustains us. To the O'Haras—not the name but the choice. The choice to stay, to build, to believe that some things are worth the beautiful terrible risk of permanence."

"To the O'Haras," everyone echoed, glasses raised.

As if the universe appreciated comic timing, Maggie launched her mashed potatoes with impressive accuracy, hitting cousin Liam square in the face. Within seconds, the younger cousins had turned dinner into performance art.

"And that," Mick said without missing a beat, "is why we keep having babies. To remind us that chaos is sacred and dignity is vastly overrated."

The meal descended into its familiar symphony—conversations layering like instruments, children needing everything simultaneously, dogs positioning themselves with strategic hope. Through it all, Dylan felt the belonging she'd never known to want washing over her like warm rain.

Outside, the storm intensified, sealing them in. The farmhouse creaked and settled—the ancient boiler complaining, the floors announcing every footstep, the bones of a house that had grown room by room with love and need.

"Next year," Anne said, surveying the chaos of her kitchen, "I'm definitely renovating."

"Twentieth year you've said that," Duncan pointed out.

"And you all keep coming anyway," she

replied, but her smile said she wouldn't change a single worn board.

As coffee replaced wine and dessert emerged despite the ancient oven's best efforts, Dylan found herself at the front window where the Christmas tree presided. Snow had erased the world beyond the ranch, turning everything into possibility.

"Perfect?" Aidan appeared at her shoulder, Maggie sleeping in his arms.

"Perfect," Dylan confirmed, leaning into his warmth.

She thought about Pinnacle Restoration, two years of bringing dead things back to life. About the woman she'd been—running from grief, building walls like they could keep loss at bay. About Patrick O'Hara's treasure hunt that had really been about teaching them both to stay still long enough to be found.

"Your grandfather knew," she said quietly. "The whole elaborate hunt—he knew exactly what would happen."

"That we'd almost freeze to death on Eagle's Point?"

"That we'd both find what we needed."

The ring caught the tree lights, centuries of promises made tangible. Through the window, snow continued its patient work, transforming the harsh into the gentle.

This was what she'd run from—not pain but the possibility of joy so complete that losing it would destroy her. But here, surrounded by O'Haras who'd claimed her before she'd known she wanted to be claimed, she understood that some things were worth the terrible beautiful risk.

"No regrets?" Aidan asked, their old refrain.

"None," Dylan said, and meant it down to her bones.

The storm would pass. Roads would clear. Everyone would scatter after a few days—Duncan to his studio, Sophie to The Reading Nook with its salvaged stained-glass window, Raven to her boutique, Colt to his medical practice, Dylan to Pinnacle Restoration where broken things learned to sing again.

But tonight, sealed in by weather and warmed by love that had survived everything from outlaws to harsh Montana winters, Dylan O'Hara understood that home wasn't a place you found but a choice you made, over and over, until the choosing became as natural as breathing.

The farmhouse settled around them with the satisfaction of walls that had heard a hundred years of Christmas Eves, of foundations that went deeper than stone, of rooms added like promises kept.

Forever, she thought, and for the first time in her life, the word felt like a beginning.

SOPHIE JACOBS LOVED CHRISTMAS.

She loved looking through the plate-glass window of her bookshop and seeing snow flurries dance to the ground, their delicate patterns illuminated by the antique gas lanterns that lined Main Street. She loved the scents of cinnamon that drifted down from Heaven's Delight Bakery and the fresh pine from the boughs that hung above the doors of all the businesses in downtown Laurel Valley. Most of all, she loved the spirit of Christmas—the good cheer, the joy, and that giving was worth more than receiving.

The Reading Nook stood like a proud sentinel on its hilltop, overlooking the Bavarian-inspired village that had grown into a thriving resort town over the past decade. Unlike the perfectly maintained alpine facades of the other buildings—with their ornate trim, flower boxes, and painted shutters—her bookstore was housed in a three-story white clapboard Victorian with a widow's walk and a round stained-glass window at the highest peak. It didn't fit with the town's carefully curated aesthetic, but it had been there long before the historical society had ever drafted their first building code.

So she couldn't figure out why Hank O'Hara was standing in her crowded store, seeming larger than life in his boots and rugged lambskin coat, asking if she had a few minutes to talk. No she didn't have a few minutes to talk. Couldn't he see that both cash registers were three people deep?

Or that Julie Milton's little boy had just knocked over a display of handcrafted beeswax candles she'd imported from Vermont? Or that Freddie, her part-time clerk, looked like she was coming down with a cold and would probably have to be sent home soon?

The worn oak floorboards creaked beneath her feet as she moved back to the counter, the sound blending with the soft instrumental Christmas music playing through hidden speakers. Every corner of the bookstore had been transformed for the season—pine garlands draped along the built-in bookshelves, vintage ornaments hanging from the ceiling beams, and a massive Fraser fir by the fireplace, adorned with tiny lights and miniature book ornaments.

She felt her perpetual Christmas cheer beginning to dim, so she kicked her smile up a notch as she tied a big red bow on one of the specialty cloth bags she sent home with shoppers, and then she handed it to the woman across the counter. She was obviously a tourist—a wealthy one judging by her designer purse and shoes that would have paid all her employees' salaries for the month—and she had the look of a woman who lived a resort lifestyle. She was probably mid-fifties, but her plastic surgeon had done a great job of putting her back in her thirties. Sophie had gotten good at pegging people quickly over the years.

And though Laurel Valley was swamped with tourists just like the woman in front of her during the Christmas season, there was no way The Reading Nook could have survived without the tourists, so she thanked God for each and every one of them.

"Merry Christmas," Sophie said. "Come back and see us."

"Thank you," the woman said, brushing artfully tousled blond bangs out of her eyes. "I just love your shop. It's so quaint. It's like it's from a different time. All these built-in bookcases and the big stained-glass window. It reminds me of my parents' home back in Ohio. My father was a carpenter. He did beautiful woodwork like this."

Sophie's gaze drifted momentarily to the grand staircase that led to the second floor, with its hand-carved newel posts and balusters. The woodwork throughout the building told a story of craftsmanship that had become rare in the age of mass production. The shelves were arranged to create cozy nooks where readers could lose themselves among the pages, and the reading chairs—placed strategically near the south-facing windows—caught the winter sunlight perfectly.

"This was the house my grandmother grew up in," Sophie said, smiling. "Her father built it. After she and my grandfather got married she used this house to open the bookstore. And then it passed to my mother. And now it's mine."

"That's wonderful," the woman said, her face lighting up with pleasure. "Merry Christmas to you." And then she headed out the door, causing the little brass bell to ring and a smattering of snow flurries to swirl onto the entry mat where they melted quickly.

Hank O'Hara was the next customer in line, and Sophie felt her smile dim. He didn't have anything in his hands, and she found herself looking at them as he laid them flat on her counter. Working man's hands. There was an interesting and jagged scar across the top of his right hand that stood out stark against his tanned skin, but otherwise his hands were unadorned.

She knew Hank, of course. Everyone in town knew the O'Haras. But she didn't know him well. Sophie had been in the same grade as his brother Wyatt, but Hank had graduated several years ahead of them. Then he'd gone off to Denver for college to get a business degree, and when he'd come home he'd opened O'Hara Construction. A lot had changed in Laurel Valley in the ten years since. He'd somehow gone from renovating the storefronts downtown, to opening multimillion-dollar ski resorts on the mountain.

The changes in Laurel Valley, whether you loved them or hated them, had everything to do with the man standing in front of her. The sleepy mountain town that had once struggled to keep its shops open past Labor Day was now a year-round destination. The old mining trails had been transformed into world-class ski runs, and luxury lodges now dotted the mountainside where cattle had once grazed. The charming Bavarian village that had once been little more than a few blocks of family-owned shops had expanded to accommodate boutiques selling designer clothing and fine jewelry—shops frequented by people who arrived in private jets at the newly expanded airport just outside town.

"Sophie Jacobs," Hank said, giving her the trademark O'Hara grin. "You're a difficult woman to get in touch with."

"Not so much," she said, her eyes skimming the shop to make sure everything was all right and none of her employees needed help. "I'm here every day. Except Sundays."

She had to give it to the O'Haras. They all had charm in spades, and none of them were hard on the eyes. But by her way of thinking, Hank had always had something a little more than the others. He was tall, a couple of inches over six feet. His shoulders were broad, and she knew under the bulky coat he wore his muscles were well defined. She'd seen him swinging a hammer or operating a heavy piece of machinery on more than one occasion. His dark-blond hair was in need of a trim and there was a scruff of beard on his face that seemed to emphasize the angle of his jaw.

But it was his eyes that held the real power. A soft green the color of the antique glass her mother liked to collect. It was rare not to see other shades of color or variation, but his were crystal clear and seemed all the more captivating framed by dark lashes.

But the Jacobses and the O'Haras didn't run in the same circles. Not by a long shot. The O'Haras were like royalty in Laurel Valley. Their ranch on the outskirts of town had been in the family for generations, and they owned half the businesses in the square. And the Jacobses...well, the Jacobses' claim to fame was that her father had driven off the mountain in a drunken stupor and the explosion had lit up the whole town. She'd been fifteen at the time. The Jacobses and the O'Haras were not the same.

"How's your family?" he asked, because that's the first thing any local asked another out of politeness.

"Good," Sophie said. "I'm meeting Mom, Aunt Lori, and Junie at The Lampstand for dinner. Apparently Mom has big news. She seemed excited."

"I'm glad to hear it," he said. "She was always nice to us when we came in here when I was a kid. I'm sure it was nerve-wracking having five boys come through here like bulls in a china shop."

"It's all part of being a shop owner," Sophie said, wincing as she heard something fall from the back. Through the arched doorway that led to the children's section, she could see Freddie hurrying to pick up a display of holiday pop-up books that had toppled. "Are you buying something?"

"No," he said, grinning again. "I figured waiting in line was the only way I'd get to talk to you. I've been trying to reach you for a couple of weeks."

"It's the busiest season of the year," she said, not meeting his gaze. Those eyes were just too unsettling, and she'd be darned if she went around fawning like other women who said one look at those eyes made them fall in love. Those women needed to have a little self-respect. And self-control. "Maybe after New Year."

"I was thinking breakfast. Before the shop opens in the morning. Say around eight o'clock?" He handed her a business card. "That's my personal cell number there."

"I don't understand," she said, turning the card over in her hand. "What's this about? Why do you want to meet?"

"I want to buy your shop," he said.

Her gaze snapped up to his and she met those cool green eyes with fire.

"I was wondering if you were ever going to look me in the eye," he said, seemingly unfazed. "Do I make you nervous?"

She could feel the anger boiling inside her, and she knew her cheeks were flushed. She sputtered. "You want to buy my shop? You must be crazy. It's not for sale."

He just smiled affably, as if they were talking about nothing more important than the weather. She noticed the little dimple at the corner of his mouth, and that he seemed to be unbothered by her anger.

"My youngest brother used to talk about you," he said, changing the subject so fast she thought she might have whiplash. "His whole junior year all he talked about was how Sophie Jacobs was the most beautiful girl in school, but he said what impressed him the most was when you stood up in the middle of English class and went toe to toe with old Mr. Fortmeyer on how Shakespeare wrote weak male characters who were useless and whiny, and that he would never make you believe that they were heroes when it was obvious it was the women he wrote who had real substance. I never liked Mr. Fortmeyer."

"What?" she asked. "That was more than ten years ago. Have you gone looney in the head?"

He just chuckled. "My brothers might tell you I have. But last time I checked I'm right as rain."

A woman peeked around Hank with eyes as wide as an owl, and her mouth opened in a little O of surprise.

"Hey, Shannon," Sophie said. "Come on up and put those on the counter. Looks like you've got a haul."

"You sure?" Shannon asked, already moving to put her items on the counter. "I don't want to interrupt."

Of course you do, Sophie thought. She and

Shannon had gone to school together, but they'd never run in the same circles. Shannon was a notorious gossip, and there was no doubt in her mind that Shannon had heard every word Hank had spoken to her and couldn't wait to spread the news. By nightfall, every patron at Duffey's Tavern would be speculating about what Hank O'Hara wanted with Sophie Jacobs' bookstore.

"Not at all," Sophie said, feeling her lungs deflate in resignation.

"Hey, Shannon," Hank said casually, moving to the side so she could maneuver around him. "How's Drew?"

Shannon looked back and forth between the two as if she wanted to tell them to go ahead and continue their previous conversation but instead she said, "He's working double shifts at the ski lodge up until the week before Christmas. It's that time of year. We rented a place down in San Diego with Drew's parents, so we're going to spend Christmas there. I think Drew needs a break from the snow before ski season starts."

"Can't say I blame him," Hank said. "He's the best ski instructor on the mountain. A couple of my brothers went out heli-skiing with him last year. They said it was amazing."

Shannon rolled her eyes. "He lives for that

stuff. Too adventurous for my blood. He does nothing but talk about getting off the mountain during the busy season, and then as soon as we're gone he can't wait to get back."

"Hank, I'm really busy today," Sophie interrupted, giving Shannon's purchases her full attention. "I'm sure you have lots of other things to do."

"I've got a few things on my plate," he said genially. "I don't want to interrupt your work."

She almost said, "Too late," but she was able to bite back the retort in time.

The gossip mill would already be going into overtime. There was no reason to add fuel to the fire by letting Shannon think there was something going on between her and Hank O'Hara. The whole idea was preposterous. The two of them had never spoken more than a couple dozen words to each other in her whole life.

Hank just grinned and then winked at Shannon. "She's a prickly one."

Shannon preened and then flirted shamelessly. "I can see she's just crazy about you."

"Tell your family hello for me and Merry Christmas," Sophie said to Hank pointedly. She bagged up Shannon's books and added the red bow on top, aware that every eye in the store seemed to be watching their interaction.

"Oh, I will," Hank said, his grin growing even wider. "See you for breakfast in the morning at eight. Let's meet at the tree. I like sitting outside, and the snow should hold off until the afternoon."

And then he turned around and walked out of her shop like he hadn't just upended her entire world. The bell over the door jangled merrily as he stepped outside, his tall frame momentarily blocking the winter light before the door swung shut behind him.

Shannon cocked her hand on her hip and pursed her lips. If she'd had on a cheerleading uniform and had been holding a pom-pom she'd have looked exactly like she had in high school. Shannon had always been a little dramatic. "What was all that about? You're having breakfast with Hank O'Hara? When did that start?"

"It started never," Sophie said flatly. "I am definitely not having breakfast with Hank O'Hara."

"Didn't sound that way to me," she said. "Lord, that man is fine. All of those boys are good looking, but there's just a little extra swagger in that one. He is one hundred percent man." And then Shannon saw the look on Sophie's face. "Oh, don't give me that look. I'm married. Not dead."

"I didn't say a word," Sophie said.

"You don't have to, honey," she said. "Your face says it for you. And you've got it bad." Shannon took her bag and grinned cheekily. "Enjoy your breakfast in the morning. I'm going to come back next week so I can hear all about it."

If she had breakfast with Hank O'Hara in the morning in the public square, there wouldn't be a swinging soul in Laurel Valley who didn't know about it. The only way to avoid the gossip was to not show up.

She had no time for whatever chaos Hank O'Hara wanted to bring into her life. She had a store to save.

THE WOMAN IN THE MIRROR WAS A MASTERPIECE of careful construction. Raven O'Hara studied her reflection with clinical detachment, noting how the mascara made her lashes sweep dramatically above crystalline blue eyes, how the hint of blush warmed her olive complexion to a sun-kissed glow, how the perfectly shaped brows framed a face that belonged on a magazine cover rather than in a mountain resort town.

Perfect. Pristine. A beautiful lie.

She'd spent thirty extra minutes on the façade this morning, layering cosmetics like an artist preparing for an exhibition. Not vanity—armor. In Laurel Valley, the O'Hara name carried weight, expectations. And the whispers—those she could already hear, ghosting through the town like autumn leaves—*Something's not right with Wyatt and Raven. Have you noticed? Have you heard?*

The motel receipt she'd found in Wyatt's jacket pocket three days ago weighed on her mind, its existence a sliver of ice lodged beneath her ribs. Mountain View Lodge, a place on the outskirts of Riverton that rented rooms by the hour. She hadn't confronted him yet—what would be the point when his answers had become as carefully constructed as her makeup?

She tucked a strand of midnight hair behind her ear, the large silver hoop earring catching the morning light that spilled through the bedroom window. The earring swung like a pendulum, marking seconds in a marriage that was crumbling with each tick forward. The delicate silver charm dangling from it—a small cactus—had been a gift from her parents when they'd moved to Arizona three years ago, seeking warmer temperatures for her father's arthritis. She missed them, especially now, and their weekly video calls were poor substitutes for the comfort of her mother's embrace or her father's steady wisdom.

"You can do this," she whispered to her reflection. "You've been doing it for months."

The thought carried no comfort, only the hollow ring of truth.

Her fingers traced the collar of her flowing maxi dress, vibrant patterns in turquoise and crimson that seemed to mock her mood with their joyful exuberance. The silk whispered against her skin as she moved, a sensual reminder of a time when touch meant connection rather than vacancy.

She inhaled deeply, the scent of her perfume—white jasmine with vanilla undertones—enveloping her in bittersweet memory. Wyatt had given her the fragrance. It was his favorite. Or it had been before everything changed.

Before the silences between them grew so vast and deep that crossing them required more courage than she could summon. Before he started coming home with that faraway look in his eyes and the smell of pine and secrets clinging to his clothes.

Her phone lay on the vanity, screen dark and accusatory. She tapped it awake, checking for messages though she already knew there would be none. Wyatt hadn't come home last night.

Again.

When had absence become their normal? When had explanations morphed into terse texts, then into nothing at all?

The sound of tires on gravel snapped her

attention toward the window. A vehicle she didn't recognize—a dark blue SUV with tinted windows—slowed as it passed their driveway, the driver's face indistinct behind the windshield. Something about the deliberate way it moved made the pulse in her neck jump with nerves. Then the SUV accelerated, continuing down the street.

She was jumping at shadows. Wyatt's absence was causing her mind to play tricks on her. She slipped her feet into strappy sandals she'd bought on her last trip to Boise with Sophie, the leather butter-soft against her skin, grabbed her car keys and purse, and then stepped out onto her front porch, closing the door behind her.

Raven closed her eyes and breathed in, letting the familiar rhythms and scents wash over her—pine and honeysuckle—the sound of a lawn-mower starting up at the end of the street—and the sunlight as it poured over the mountains like warm honey, gilding the pines and aspens that surrounded Laurel Valley.

Summer had brought the tourists—more than the summers of the past it seemed—their eager faces and expensive outdoor gear a welcome infusion to the local economy. Fortunately, the extra business meant she had more than enough to occupy her mind.

This was Laurel Valley.

Home. Community. The web of connections that had held her steady through every storm of her life.

Except this one. This storm lived inside her own house, her own marriage.

"Enough," she said aloud, the word sharp in the quiet room.

The drive into town took exactly seven minutes, a journey so familiar she could navigate it blindfolded. Each curve and dip in the road mapped not just in her mind but in her muscle memory.

Downtown Laurel Valley looked like it had been plucked straight from a tourism brochure—charming chalets with flower boxes spilling geraniums and petunias in riotous bloom, cobblestone streets polished by decades of footfalls, and the majestic Twin Peaks standing sentinel in the background. She could almost hear the background music that should accompany such a scene.

Raven turned her car into the small employee parking lot behind The Reading Nook, the renovated bookstore that had risen from the ashes last year like a phoenix. Sophie and Hank had poured not just money but heart into ensuring the rebuilt store maintained the charm of the original while adding modern amenities, including the stained-glass window salvaged from the fire, which now cast rainbow patterns across the wooden floors inside.

As she pulled into her usual spot, she noticed Sophie's hybrid with its trunk open, stacks of boxes visible inside. Sophie herself was precariously balancing a tower of hardcovers while trying to reach for another box, her petite frame barely visible behind the stack. The scene pulled a genuine smile from Raven—the first of the day.

Sophie's wild wavy hair bounced with each movement, the rich brown catching copper highlights in the morning sun. The woman was perpetual motion contained in five feet two inches of determination.

Raven stepped out of her car, the familiar scent of old books mingling with fresh coffee from the café next door. "Need a hand before you become a bookstore casualty?" she called.

Sophie peered around her tower of books, her expressive brown eyes lighting up with relief.

"My hero!" she exclaimed, the stack wobbling dangerously as she shifted. "June's book club selections arrived, and I swear they multiply when I'm not looking. I swear if I have to read one more novel about a woman finding herself in Tuscany,

I'm going to book a one-way ticket there just to spite the authors."

Raven hurried over, taking half the stack from Sophie's arms, feeling the comforting weight of the books in her hands.

"Thanks for the rescue," Sophie said. "I was about ten seconds away from a literary avalanche."

The banter felt normal, grounding. For a moment, Raven could pretend that the rest of her life felt equally solid.

They maneuvered the books to the back door of the shop, where Sophie balanced her stack precariously with one hand while fishing for her keys with the other.

"How do you have this much energy this early?" Raven asked. "Please tell me you're hiding gallons of caffeine somewhere in your bag."

"I got my fix from The Lampstand," Sophie said, finally getting the door open with a triumphant "Ha!" that echoed in the alley. "Simone's experimenting with some new hazelnut blend that might actually be worth committing minor crimes for. I can send Freddie to grab you one if you've got time."

Raven set the books down on the counter just inside the doorway, inhaling the scent of paper and possibility that defined The Reading Nook. Sophie had created a haven here—books organized by mood rather than strict alphabetical order, reading nooks tucked into corners with plush chairs that invited lingering, and always, always, fresh flowers by the register.

"I should probably get to the boutique," Raven said, regret genuine in her voice. "New summer shipment arrived yesterday, and if I don't get those sundresses displayed, how will the tourists know they absolutely need them?"

Sophie set her own stack down and turned, studying Raven's face with the perceptive gaze that made her both a wonderful friend and occasionally unnerving companion. Her expression shifted from playful to concerned in the space of a heartbeat. "Everything okay? You've got your 'I'm fine' face on, but your eyes are doing that thing."

"What thing?" Raven asked, instantly defensive, one hand rising to touch her carefully applied eye makeup.

"That sad sparkly thing, like you're two seconds from either crying or stabbing someone with your earrings." Sophie's voice gentled, though her gaze remained steady. "You don't have to talk about it, but I'm here if you need to."

The genuine concern in Sophie's voice nearly

broke through Raven's carefully constructed façade. For a fleeting moment, she considered unburdening herself—telling Sophie about the late nights, the unexplained absences, the growing suspicion that Wyatt was keeping something from her. Something big enough to drive a wedge between them.

The words hovered, dangerous and tempting, on the tip of her tongue.

Wyatt had been honest about his DEA work when they first met—it was part of what had drawn her to him, his dedication to stopping the flow of drugs into communities like Laurel Valley. But the "consulting" jobs Blaze had brought him in on recently had transformed into something else entirely. The "overtime" work had gradually consumed him, leaving less and less of the man she'd married.

The trust between them, once as solid as the mountains that cradled their town, had developed hairline fractures that threatened to become chasms.

"Just tired. Inventory season, you know?" she said instead, offering a bright smile that felt stretched too thin across her face. "Nothing a gallon of coffee and some retail therapy won't fix."

Sophie didn't look convinced. Her eyes—warm brown and too perceptive by half—narrowed slightly, but she nodded, respecting the boundary Raven had drawn. "Well, my door's always open. And I've got wine in the back office for emergencies." She paused, then added, "Whatever's going on, Raven, you're not alone in it. Remember that."

The simple assurance wrapped around Raven like a quilt on a winter night, unexpected warmth when she'd been braced for cold.

"I know," she said, squeezing Sophie's arm gratefully, the connection of skin on skin a reminder of the bonds that existed beyond her troubled marriage. "Rain check on that coffee? I promise I'll swing by later."

"I'll hold you to that," Sophie said, turning to go back to her car for more books, her movements efficient despite her small stature.

As Raven walked the short distance to her boutique, she felt both lighter and heavier. The warmth of friendship was a comfort, but it also highlighted what was missing at home. She glanced at her phone again—still no message from Wyatt. The screen remained stubbornly, accusingly blank.

For a brief moment, a prickling sensation

crept up the back of her neck, that peculiar feeling of being watched. Her pulse quickened as her gaze swept the plaza, landing on a man in expensive hiking gear sitting at one of the outdoor café tables.

He appeared absorbed in his phone and coffee, the mirrored sunglasses perched on his nose reflecting the morning light. Nothing unusual about that—tourists in performance outerwear that had never seen a trail were commonplace in Laurel Valley this time of year.

When she looked more closely, she realized he wasn't even facing her direction. The breath she hadn't realized she was holding escaped in a soft sigh. She shook her head slightly, annoyed at her own paranoia. The strain in her marriage was clearly affecting her in ways she hadn't anticipated, making her jumpy and suspicious of ordinary tourists enjoying their vacations.

With practiced movements, she unlocked the front door of Raven Layne Boutique and stepped inside. The familiar scent of her shop—a mixture of fine fabrics, subtle designer perfume, and the essential oils she diffused—welcomed her in, wrapping around her like an embrace.

Here, at least, she knew exactly who she was and what she was doing. Here, luxury fabrics and exclusive designs obeyed her direction, inventory from Milan and Paris arrived when scheduled, and elite clientele responded predictably to her carefully curated collections. Here, she was still fully herself—Raven Layne, businesswoman, fashion curator, the woman who had created a destination that both locals and wealthy visitors sought out for statement pieces they couldn't find elsewhere.

She ran her fingers across a display of imported silk scarves, each one selected for its exquisite craftsmanship and luxurious feel. This space was a reflection of her vision, her impeccable taste, her understanding of what affluent visitors to Laurel Valley desired when they stepped off the slopes and into her high-end boutique.

The boutique was her creation, as solid and true as her marriage had once been.

As she moved toward the back office to prepare for opening, her phone buzzed in her pocket. She pulled it out, heart leaping with stupid, stubborn hope.

A text from Wyatt. Finally.

Catching a few hours sleep. See you later. - W

Eight words. Eight cold, impersonal words that told her nothing and everything at the same time. No endearment. No explanation. Just a notification, as if she were his secretary instead of his wife.

Raven set the phone face-down on the counter, refusing to let the tears gathering behind her eyes fall. The rest of her life might be a mystery, but for the next ten hours, she could lose herself in the rhythm of commerce and the comfort of beautiful things. It was enough.

It had to be.

Liliana Hart is a *New York Times*, *USA Today*, and Publisher's Weekly bestselling author of more than eighty titles. After starting her first novel her freshman year of college, she immediately became addicted to writing and knew she'd found what she was meant to do with her life. She has no idea why she majored in music.

Since publishing in June 2011, Liliana has sold more than ten-million books. All three of her series have made multiple appearances on the New York Times list.

Liliana can almost always be found at her computer writing, hauling five kids to various activities, or spending time with her husband. She calls Texas home.

If you enjoyed reading this book, I would appreciate it if you would help others enjoy this book too.

Recommend it. Please help other readers find this book by recommending it to friends, readers' groups and discussion boards.

Review it. Please tell other readers why you liked this book by reviewing.

Connect with me online:
www.lilianahart.com

Also by Liliana Hart

JJ Graves Mystery Series

Dirty Little Secrets

A Dirty Shame

Dirty Rotten Scoundrel

Down and Dirty

Dirty Deeds

Dirty Laundry

Dirty Money

A Dirty Job

Dirty Devil

Playing Dirty

Dirty Martini

Dirty Dozen

Dirty Minds

Dirty Weekend

Dirty Looks

Dirty Liars

Dirty Valentine

Addison Holmes Mystery Series

Whiskey Rebellion

Whiskey Sour

Whiskey For Breakfast

Whiskey, You're The Devil

Whiskey on the Rocks

Whiskey Tango Foxtrot

Whiskey and Gunpowder

Whiskey Lullaby

The Scarlet Chronicles

Bouncing Betty

Hand Grenade Helen

Front Line Francis

The Harley and Davidson Mystery Series

The Farmer's Slaughter

A Tisket a Casket

I Saw Mommy Killing Santa Claus

Get Your Murder Running

Deceased and Desist

Malice in Wonderland

Tequila Mockingbird

Gone With the Sin

Grime and Punishment

Blazing Rattles

A Salt and Battery

Curl Up and Dye

First Comes Death Then Comes Marriage

Box Set 1

Box Set 2

Box Set 3

The Gravediggers

The Darkest Corner

Gone to Dust

Say No More

Laurel Valley

Tribulation Pass

Redemption Road

Midnight Clear

Forgiveness River

Atonement Trail

www.ingramcontent.com/pod-product-compliance
Lightning Source LLC
Chambersburg PA
CBHW061234310726
48971CB00007B/2065